GODS OF THE DAWN

GODS
OF
THE
DAWN

The Message of the Pyramids
and the True Stargate Mystery

Peter Lemesurier

Thorsons
An Imprint of HarperCollins*Publishers*

R0128880043

Thorsons

An Imprint of HarperCollins*Publishers*

77–85 Fulham Palace Road,

Hammersmith, London W6 8JB

Published by Thorsons 1998

1 3 5 7 9 10 8 6 4 2

Stargate is a trademark of Le Studio Canal (U.S.)

Peter Lemesurier asserts the moral right to
be identified as the author of this work

A catalogue record for this book
is available from the British Library

ISBN 0 7225 3549 X

Printed and bound in Great Britain by
Creative Print and Design (Wales), Ebbw Vale

CONTENTS

The Great Pyramid is a symbol of a
now almost wholly alien mentality.

Arthur C. Clarke, *Profiles of the Future*

FOREWORD

TRUTH, IT HAS BEEN SAID, IS STRANGER THAN FICTION. And so when two major theories converge to identify the pyramids of Giza in Egypt as elements of an ancient star-map – a map designed by who knows whom to grab our collective attention and summon us to the stars – it is perhaps no surprise to be reminded of the fictional *2001: A Space Odyssey* and the equally fictional *Stargate*.

Yet this is no fiction. The geographical facts that underlie Robert Bauval's star-map theory are no less serious than the geometrical and trigonometrical data that underlie my own read-out of the Great Pyramid's internal passages and chambers, arrived at some six years before.

Together, they make a pair. Together, too, they face us with a mystery – and a challenge.

What mighty race was it that bequeathed to us this colossal route-map to the stars? What intelligence conceived the idea of memorializing its vital passage-directions to us in enduring stone monuments of such cyclopean immensity? How are we to respond? Where are we expected to head?

And why?

To many, the very suggestion even that there *is* a message in the stones may seem startling. That it takes the form suggested in this book may seem unimaginable. That our collective destiny is of the order suggested may seem laughable.

Yet the facts are there, too vast to expunge, too huge to erase. Make of them what we will, they cannot be ignored.

And perhaps it is the gods who are laughing.

1

THE
CHANGING
PAST

THE HISTORY OF HISTORY HOLDS an awful warning for us – a warning that things may be very much other than we currently believe.

Until only a couple of centuries ago, after all, Christendom was confident that it knew the date of Creation itself. The world had begun, it was perfectly clear, in around 4000 BC. The exact date admittedly varied. The French doctor, astronomer, mathematician and seer Michel Nostradamus, writing in the middle of the 16th century, seems to have offered three different figures for it in the selfsame document[30] – namely 4757, 4657 and 4173 BC – a fact which might suggest that any datings attached to his subsequent predictions should be taken with at least a pinch of salt. Archbishop James Ussher of Armagh, writing in the middle of the 17th, more confidently (and famously) narrowed it down to a single year – 4004 BC – and not just to any old date, either, but to 22 October, at six o'clock in the evening.[40]

To this day, many fundamentalist Christians believe much the same. The general unanimity is unsurprising, since the common source of it all is the familiar Bible. This specifically lists the generations of humanity right back to the beginning, often giving their exact ages. Consequently calculating the time back to the Creation is not a problem, give or take a disputed interpretation or two.

Yet if the Bible is to be regarded as history – i.e. as written evidence for what has occurred in the past – and if the Bible also records the very Creation itself, there is an important corollary. *It is that, on this model, the date of Creation and the date of the beginning of history are identical.*

Prehistory, in short, does not exist.

About 150 years after Archbishop Ussher's astonishing calculation, however, worrying things started to happen. Canal builders such as William Smith started to realize that the rock strata through which they were driving their new cuttings not only contained a whole variety of strange, fossilized creatures – many of them previously unknown – but also displayed a clearly defined sequence that was more or less constant everywhere. Indeed, the fossils could actually be used to identify the strata.[38] Smith's work in fact laid the foundations for what is now known as geology.

Among those fossils, too, was something even more worrying, as the Frenchman Georges Cuvier was soon to discover. It was thanks to the exploratory work of this eminent zoologist that humanity now came suddenly and dramatically face to face with the ancient dinosaurs – which was something that (as subsequent research was to reveal) it had certainly not done in the creatures' day.

Smith's literally ground-breaking book, meanwhile, was followed within only a couple of decades by Charles Lyell's seminal *Principles of Geology* (1830 onwards), in which the Oxford botanist advanced a variety of techniques both geological and botanical for actually *dating* the formation of the strata. The book profoundly influenced the theologian and naturalist Charles Darwin, whose celebrated *Origin of Species* of 1859 did even more to put the final bomb under the old notions of chronology.

The Earth, it seemed, was far older than the mere 6000 years that had previously been assumed. It was immeasurably, unimaginably old. The rock strata had been laid down over not just thousands, but hundreds of millions of years. Nothing else could

Present

200 million years ago	Cenozoic	Quaternary	Man, apes, mammals and plants	Historical era
		Tertiary	Monkeys, early mammals, insects, specialized birds	
	Mesozoic	Cretaceous	Giant reptiles & dinosaurs, pterosaurs, ichthyosaurs; birds; small mammals	
		Jurassic	Dinosaurs, archaeopteryx, diplodocus, early mammals	
		Triassic	Reptiles, small dinosaurs, pterodactyls, early flies and termites, conifers	
400 million years ago	Palaeozoic	Permian	True land creatures emerge (mainly reptiles); many insects; tree ferns	
		Carboniferous	Amphibians, some land reptiles; winged insects	
		Devonian	Fishes, sharks, early amphibians, spiders, wingless insects	
		Silurian	Primitive fishes, crustaceans, corals	
		Ordovician	Marine invertebrates, seaweeds	
		Cambrian	Worms, trilobites, sponges	
600 million years ago	Upper Proterozoic	Pre-Cambrian	Little life, mostly protozoic	

The ages of the Earth: the geological record
Datings are very approximate

possibly explain their sequence, their deformations, the distribution and gradual mutations of the fossils they contained.

Nothing, that is, except some extraordinary and wilful act of Divine magic perpetrated for no better reason than to fool the latter-day investigators.

More recently, other techniques – notably the measuring of residual radioactivity – have helped to refine the process even further. The Earth, according to current estimates, is now some *4,700 million* years old.

But if the Creation of the world has had to be pushed back nearly five thousand million years, and that of the universe itself some three or four times further back still – for modern 'expanding universe' theorists still seem determined to maintain something extraordinarily akin to the Creation theory through thick and thin, whatever the evidence to the contrary[18] – then something pretty catastrophic has happened.

Creation and history have finally parted company.

Historians, after all, continue to this day to maintain that history began in the fourth millennium BC. True, agricultural technology was evidently developing and spreading as early as 9000 BC, while some kind of city was flourishing at Jericho as early as 8000 BC. Recognizable writing, however, did not appear on the scene in the Middle East until 4000–3000 BC – and without writing there is of course no history. Before that there are only rumour, myth, superstition, tall tales of dubious pedigree and speculative reconstructions based on non-literary sources. Before that, in short, there is only *pre*history – a prehistory that only archaeologists can hope to decipher.

A prehistory that, on this model, is supposed to cover the whole of the Earth's existence apart from the last few ticks of the geological clock (*see diagram above*).

It is difficult to over-stress the point. *For the historian, everything of note (and I stress the word 'note') that has ever happened has done so in the last six thousand years. In all the long aeons before that, nothing historical is supposed to have happened – nothing recordable, nothing reported – for literally millions of years.*

4

It is an astonishing idea – so astonishing, in fact, that most historians are totally unaware of how astonishing it really is. It is only specialists in other fields who, agog at the enormity of the idea, continually suggest a whole range of apparently 'historical' events that predate orthodox history by whole millennia.

The historians, naturally, are somewhat piqued by such suggestions. Indeed, they typically treat them as tantamount to heresy (which is always, of course, a sure sign of the presence of dogma). 'Who are these people?' they tend to ask. 'What do they know about history?' And, more to the point, 'Where is the evidence?'

The implication is of course that, *given* the evidence, the historians might be persuaded to change their minds and accept the broader view.

Studiously ignoring the first two questions, the non-specialists have therefore duly produced what they assume *to be* the evidence. Among the items they offer are:

- The Maya and Aztecs, who calculated dates as much as 300 million years into the past, asserted that the world had known four whole ages *before* the present one, whose beginning they dated to 3114 BC.[13, 19]
  'Primitive superstition,' say the historians.
- The ancient Hindu scriptures known as the *Puranas* claim that humanity is now in the early stages of the last of *four* ages, the first of which started some four million years ago.[23]
  'Mere priestly speculation,' say the historians.
- As keeper of records to the Ptolemies Soter and Philadelphus (323–247 BC), the Egyptian priest Manetho asserted that Egyptian civilization had existed for 36,525 years prior to the end of the 30th dynasty in 332 BC – and he left behind him actual records in his *Egyptian History* to prove it. The work disappeared in around the 9th century AD, but reports of it (including some direct quotations) have come down to us in various editions, notably those of Africanus (4th century), Eusebius (4th century) and George Syncellus (9th century), even though not all of their figures agree.[13, 19] The even more

ancient *Turin Papyrus* (13th century BC) offers similarly mind-boggling figures, *while a good many of Manetho's actually seem to have been built into the dimensions of the Great Pyramid itself*, so fixing them for ever in stone.[19]

'Priestly yarn-spinning and numerophilia,' say the historians.

- The revered Athenian sage, lawgiver and statesman Solon (c. 638–c. 558 BC) is reported by none other than Plato as having been told by the Egyptian priests of his day that a great civilization known as Atlantis had been overwhelmed by earthquakes and tidal waves some 9,000 years previously, and that humanity had undergone numerous other destructions before that.[17, 32]

  'Priestly superstition,' say the historians.

- The celebrated American psychic and seer Edgar Cayce (1877–1945) claimed that the Great Pyramid of Giza, Egypt, was originally built under the aegis of Atlantean colonists between 10,490 and 10,390 BC (Reading 5748–6).[19]

  'Credulous nonsense,' say the historians – or rather the Egyptologists who nowadays fulfil the role of archaeologists and historians rolled into one.

- An inscription, allegedly by the Pharaoh Khufu, on the 21st dynasty Inventory Stela, now in the Cairo Museum, records that the Great Pyramid and Sphinx were already in existence *long before* he came to the throne.[37]

  'Forged,' say the Egyptologists.

  (Quite why what is evidently a copy of an earlier inscription has to be regarded as a fake is nowhere explained. On the same basis, after all, all the world's ancient scriptures – none of which exists in original manuscript – would likewise have to be dismissed as 'forgeries'.)

The rejection by the historians of psychics such as Edgar Cayce is of course entirely understandable in view of the rationality which they like to affect. For much the same reason, the evident contempt for the word of mere priests is also understandable. But the airy dismissal of actual stone inscriptions, to say nothing of the ancient world's most eminent historians and scholars (most of whom, as

Source	Reference	Years	Application in Great Pyramid
Turin Papyrus	All dynasties to beginning of 1st	36,620	Base perimeter in primitive inches
Turin Papyrus	Shemsu-Hor (Followers of Horus)	23,200	Designed height in primitive inches
Syncellus	All dynasties to end of 30th	36,525	Circuit at 35th course axis (P")
Manetho	Dynasty of Menes	5,813	
Manetho	Gods and Kings	29,220	*Herodotus lists:*
Africanus	Divine dynasties	25,827	*8 gods*
Manetho	3rd dynasty of demigods	1,702	*12 further gods*
Africanus	Human dynasties 1 to 31	5,474	*4 dynasties of demigods*
Castor	Human dynasties 1 to 18	3,720	*30 human dynasties*
Eusebius	Human dynasties 1 to 31	4,565	Half base-side in primitive inches
Africanus	First 26 human dynasties	5,151	Side of square = area of cross-section (P")

The evidence of the Turin Papyrus and of Manetho's king-lists
the latter as edited by Africanus, Eusebius, Syncellus et al., and as reflected in the dimensions of the Great Pyramid [19]

it happens, *were* priests) is more than a little worrying. The gifted Mayan astronomers and mathematicians, the great Plato and Solon, the Egyptian archivist Manetho – all, it seems, are credulous fools, to be consigned to the same ignoble dustbin.

Which is odd, given that Manetho's chronology *after* the beginning of the dynastic period in around 3100 BC *is accepted* by the historians and Egyptologists: indeed, it forms the very basis of their understanding of Egyptian history.

One would not wish to attribute unseemly motives to them, yet it is almost as if they did not *want* to accept the rest of the evidence…

It is all rather reminiscent of the undignified squirmings of cosmologists wedded to the fashionable dogma of Big Bang and Expanding Universe, as more and more evidence comes in to cast doubt on their favourite theory. Critics such as the eminent astronomers Halton Arp and V. A. Ambartsumian are ostracized, banned, anathematized, while more and more complex sub-theories are continually developed to prop up the established dogma and tie down the new evidence, to the point where the whole edifice threatens to collapse under its own weight.[18]

But then this in turn is much like all those mountains of medieval speculation about how many angels could dance on the head of a pin – except that the medieval speculation was marginally more scientific. People, after all, had actually *seen* pins. Some of them even claimed to have seen angels…

Perhaps all this is not so very surprising. The experts have become experts by successfully regurgitating the established wisdom. They owe their positions to public funding that is awarded on the very basis of their proven expertise in the areas concerned. They are possibly the last people to whom we should look for new ideas.

Darwin, after all, was a theologian. Einstein was a clerk in the patent office at Berne at the time when he proposed his special theory of relativity. Alfred Wegener, who proposed the idea of continental drift, was not a geologist at all, but a meteorologist.

And so it is that the historians – and, with them, history itself – remain stuck within the framework of a post-biblical chronology long ago laid down by Joseph Justus Scaliger (1540–1609), the distinguished son of Nostradamus's sometime mentor at Agen. And there they are likely to stay unless and until some much more powerful evidence surfaces that finally forces their horizons apart.

But then, astonishingly enough, that is precisely what now appears to be happening…

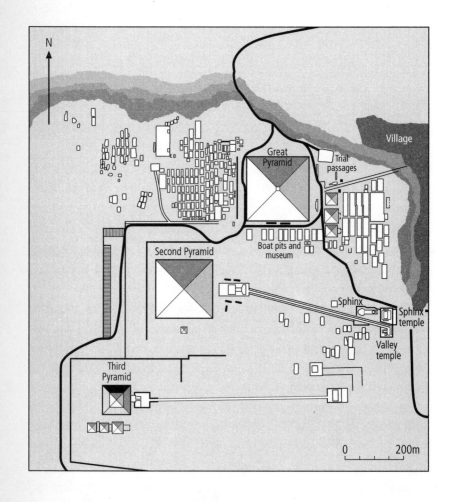

N

Village

Great
Pyramid

Trial
passages

Second Pyramid

Boat pits and
museum

Sphinx

Sphinx
temple

Valley
temple

Third
Pyramid

0   200m

The Giza complex

showing the pyramids in their presumed original state

10

2

THE
RIDDLE
OF THE
SPHINX

THE MIGHTY MONUMENT FIELD OF GIZA, just south-west of Cairo in Egypt, has accompanied humanity through most of recorded history – perhaps even (as we shall see) through all of it and more. There it has always been, for ever potentially present in our consciousness. That long familiarity has bred, if not contempt, at least bemused acceptance. What should be to us a matter of supreme mystery has become a mere matter of course.

Yet its superhuman achievement, its sheer massiveness, its lordly anonymity, its disdainful silence and above all, perhaps, its apparently sudden and anachronistic appearance amidst the gloom of primitive antiquity should inspire anything *but* acceptance in us. It should shock us, disturb us, even scare us.

What mighty civilization spawned such a huge and awe-inspiring plan? Who mapped it out, planned it, executed it? Who cut the massive stones, moved them from their quarries and laid them in place with such titanic strength and machine-like accuracy?

And above all, why?

That is the question not that we ask of it, but that *it* asks of *us*. It is the supreme and ultimate riddle of the Sphinx.

Huge and sprawling, this enormous 73-metre-long monolith, carved out of the living rock, has seemingly guarded the whole, vast complex ever since the dawn of time, its unblinking gaze fixed directly and for ever on the equinoctial sunrise. The sands have come and gone, now burying its great body to the neck, now cleared again by reverential pharaohs or latter-day public authorities. During the whole of the historical era its exposed head has been sand-blasted by the winds and (as the Inventory Stela reveals) assaulted by storms and lightning as well. Its body, though – for the most part protected by the all-enveloping sand – has suffered only about a thousand years of such treatment.

Yet the evidence now emerging suggests that there was a time, long before the coming either of the sands or of the historical era, when the whole colossus stood clear and proud amid a verdant landscape, grandiloquently surveying the flowing waters of the Nile as they performed their immemorial annual flood cycle.

In those days, though, it was a different Sphinx.

As yet unblasted by the weather, its body was much smoother, its head much larger. Probably it was the head of a lion. Certainly the current head (which, contrary to accepted tradition, looks nothing like the Pharaoh Khafre) is disproportionately small, belying the clear sense of proportion that its creators displayed in the rest of the design. Evidently the head was carved in remote antiquity out of a much more ample original that dated from an even more remote antiquity – an original that had by then become disfigured and made almost unrecognizable by the relentless onslaught of the sands of time (*see Colour Plate*).

And not only of the sands.

For the fact is that the body reveals clear evidence of *water erosion* – the result of *thousands of years of heavy rain*. To any competent geologist the evidence is quite conclusive – a fact which has of course not prevented the Egyptologists (and even a handful of geologists who would rather not have their historical preconceptions disturbed) from denying it. As the defining work of Professor Robert Schoch of Boston has confirmed,[13] the deep, undulating, vertical gulleys worn in the ancient limestone are quite definitely precipitation-induced (to quote the jargon), and totally distinct from the more general effects of simple exfoliation and the sharper-edged results of wind erosion, with its propensity simply to pick out softer areas of rock without regard to their orientation.

The same goes for the walls of the ancient rock enclosure in which the Sphinx reclines – as well as for the original walls of the Valley Temple immediately to the south-east of it, whose huge, 200-tonne blocks were originally carved out of the same enclosure. The temple walls, in fact, were *re*-lined with new, granite blocks during the Old Kingdom (roughly 2780 to 2100 BC) – *blocks that were actually contoured to fit the then already-eroded limestone masonry beneath*. Much the same goes for the Sphinx itself. In places its body, too, was faced with repair-blocks in ancient times – and here, too, the blocks were carefully contoured to fit the underlying, *already-existing* erosion.

The conclusion, then, seems inescapable – except to those who have already irrevocably drawn their conclusions and have consequently ceased to ask questions. It is that both Sphinx and Temple existed long millennia before the Old Kingdom – much as the Egyptians themselves always maintained – carved out during some earlier age before the desert and its encroaching sands overwhelmed a green and well-watered landscape on which the rains had beaten regularly for millennia.

Which is no doubt why the Inventory Stela more or less suggests as much, and why the surrounding much later Old Kingdom monuments are totally devoid of such signs of water-erosion.

The Sphinx, then, is quite simply *non-historical*. It dates not from dynastic times but from remote prehistory. The last time Egypt enjoyed a fairly rainy climate was between 7,000 and 5,000 BC. But it seems unlikely that this period of declining rainfall could have done all the damage on its own. *The only period that was wet and prolonged enough to deluge the area in the way required was the era of rain and floods that lasted from 13,000 BC to 10,000 BC.*

Here then, is solid evidence, if evidence were needed, that some highly advanced civilization did indeed exist in the area well before the historical era, just as various of the ancient sources (and not merely the modern Edgar Cayce) always maintained.

But will the historians and Egyptologists look at this evidence, let alone accept it? In all probability not. Geology, after all, is 'out of their area'. They prefer books, manuscripts, inscriptions – and preferably ones that back up their preconceptions. Much like Renaissance scholars and many Protestant theologians, they would rather believe the ancient documents than the evidence of their own eyes. At least, then, the tendency has a long and respectable pedigree.

Which is why they will no doubt reject the similarly solid evidence that is also emerging from elsewhere.

They will reject, for a start, the evidence that the ancient, circular step-pyramid of Cuicuilco, beside the road out of Mexico City to Cuernavaca, was overwhelmed by a volcanic lava-flow in around 6,500 BC – which means, of course, that it had already been there for some time before that. The fact, after all, conflicts totally with currently-accepted datings for Central American civilization – which is why historians and archaeologists generally seem too embarrassed to discuss it.[13]

They will similarly reject the clear evidence that the builders of the ancient Bolivian city of Tiahuanaco incorporated into its design – characterized by the use of stone blocks even more huge than those of the Egyptian Sphinx's Valley Temple – carvings of creatures that became extinct in around 10,000 BC as a result of some natural disaster that also overwhelmed the city itself.[13]

Which means, of course, that they will certainly reject the clear *astronomical* evidence that the city was in fact planned *as early as 15,000 BC*, as also the even more startling astronomical evidence that (as we shall see in the next chapter) has finally succeeded in dating the construction – or at least the planning – of the Giza.[13]

They will reject as heresy, in short, anything that conflicts with their current theory, especially if it bases itself on any sphere of enquiry outside their restricted expertise. It was ever so. Every new idea that conflicts with the existing corpus of beliefs is a heresy by definition. Christianity was a heresy in its day, as was Protestantism in the sixteenth century. So was the suggestion that the Earth revolved about the sun, or that meteorites fell from the sky.

Evolutionary theory was a prime heresy in the mid–19th century, and still remains so today among many fundamentalist Christians. Virtually every scientific advance since then – from continental drift to space flight itself – has been regarded as a heresy by somebody in authority. Many establishment scientists still regard as heresies all talk of extraterrestrials or faster-than-light travel – to say nothing of the possibility that the universe did not, after all, begin in a Big Bang and may not be expanding, either.[18]

Yet 'heresy' (from Greek *haeresis*) means 'choice' or 'personal opinion'. The very use of the word is a sure sign of the presence of dogma. It is a sign that questions are being asked.

And the day when we cease to ask questions is the day when we die.

THE
MAP OF
HEAVEN
ON
EARTH

THE ANCIENT CIVILIZATION THAT LEFT US the Sphinx and the Valley Temple was not content merely to dazzle us with its amazing antediluvian expertise. It was determined to tell us exactly *when* it performed its staggering feats of technical legerdemain.

It was Robert Bauval – appropriately, a construction engineer – who on a desert camping expedition late in 1983 first hit on the idea that the layout of Giza was in reality an ancient star-chart. The three major pyramids, he realized, mapped out on the ground with astonishing accuracy the slightly imperfect alignment of the three stars of Orion's Belt – Al Nitak (or Alnitak), Al Nilam (or Alnilam) and Mintaka. The nearby Nile corresponded to the adjacent Milky Way. Even the pyramids of Dashur, to the south, faithfully reflected the familiar sky-picture in the form of the stellar cluster of the Hyades.

At once, the ancient Egyptian rituals and funeral traditions started to make new sense. The great god Osiris, bringer of civilization and lord of the dead, had always been associated with Orion, just as his queen, the goddess Isis, had been associated with the star Sirius, whose heliacal rising had since time immemorial held such huge significance for the Egyptians and their calendar. The symbolic 'Waterway', counterpart of the Nile, with which his journeys in the *Duat*, or underworld, had always been associated, suddenly became a reality – for there it now flowed, pale and glowing, across the starry vault in the form of the Milky Way. And the symbolic union of Upper and Lower Kingdoms immemorially embodied by the pharaohs was now no longer a mere act of political geography, but an affirmation of the ultimate identity of heaven and Earth – an identity that had at last suddenly become starkly and physically apparent.

The alacrity with which everything now fell into place – the ancient texts, the latter-day suggestions of scholars as to their true significance – was quite astonishing. So astonishing, in fact, that Bauval would go on to publish two books on the topic in a couple of years with the aid of Adrian Gilbert (writer, publisher, and former publisher's sales representative) and journalist Graham Hancock – namely *The Orion Mystery* (Heinemann, 1994; Mandarin, 1995) and *Keeper of Genesis* (Heinemann, 1996) respectively.

There was one slight problem, however. Although the three pyramids were undoubtedly in their right places, their line, relative to the Nile, was skewed anticlockwise by some 37° when compared with the picture in the sky. But the reason for this turned out to be perfectly logical. As a result of equinoctial precession, the orientation of the stars in the sky had gradually changed over the centuries. Thanks to the advent of modern computer technology, it was now possible to unwind the celestial clock until the stellar alignment fitted the alignment on the ground.

Bauval and his colleagues duly performed the operation. The result was stunning. *Perfect alignment was finally achieved in 10,500 BC* – almost exactly the year pinpointed by Edgar Cayce for the beginning of work on the original Great Pyramid (*see Chapter 1*).

But there were further bonuses. For the vernal sun, as I myself pointed out some 20 years ago,[19] was in the constellation Leo at the time. At the equinoctial sunrise, therefore, the leonine Sphinx, which faces due east, would have been pointing directly at the area of its celestial counterpart, which would by this juncture be

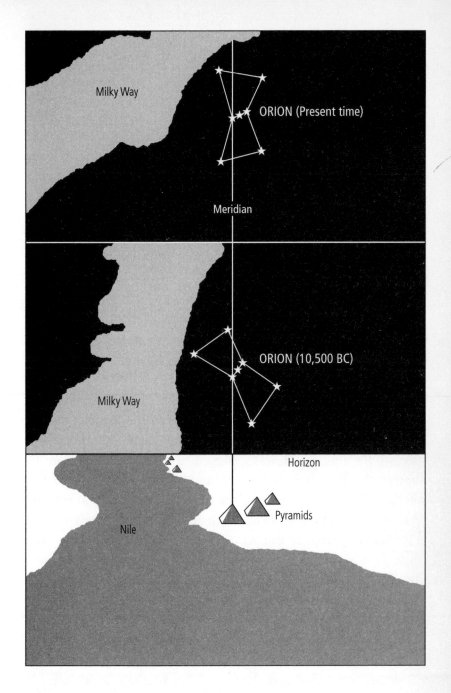

Milky Way

ORION (Present time)

Meridian

Milky Way

ORION (10,500 BC)

Horizon

Pyramids

Nile

The Pyramids of Giza and the stars of Orion's belt
Artist's impression after Bauval and Hancock[2]

some 12 degrees above the horizon. That, no doubt, was why it was constructed in the form of a lion in the first place.

At the same moment, meanwhile, the belt of Orion was passing directly through the southern meridian, and at the very lowest point of its slow, 26,000-year precessional cycle. At this selfsame moment, too, the goddess-star Sirius was rising in the south-east.

The Lion rising. Osiris at his daily culmination, and yet at the lowest point in his age-long pilgrimage. Isis awakening with the dawn. This – there could no longer be any doubt about it – was the awesome *Zep Tepi* repeatedly referred to by the ancient texts: it was the First Time, the beginning of all things, the start of the mighty cycle.

A cycle whose culmination – the Last Time, the high-point of Orion, the final triumph of Osiris – would not be reached until around 2450 AD.

But what did all this mean? Who had chosen to mark their presence so emphatically in this way and to pinpoint their initiative so precisely in time? What was their message? What was their purpose?

Here Bauval and his colleagues were less sure. Certainly the Giza was set up as some kind of marker for future generations. By dint of its sheer massiveness, it was designed to last. Having successfully done so, it was designed to grab their attention, to impress them with its titanic technology, to assure them that somebody had been here long before. Perhaps, too, it was intended to remind them that life on Earth, and human life in particular, is intimately geared to the great cosmic clock itself, and that it is consequently subject to all the effects – whether ice ages, seismic disturbances or other major events – that the Earth's precessional cycle brings with it.

True, the causes of Ice Ages are as yet imperfectly understood. They may be caused by anything from interstellar dust, through precessional tilting, to periodic displacements of the Earth's crust resulting in a repositioning of the poles.[11] But 10,500 BC, certainly, fell not long after the last of them. Sea levels worldwide were still rising as the ice melted. Low-lying lands were being flooded one by one.

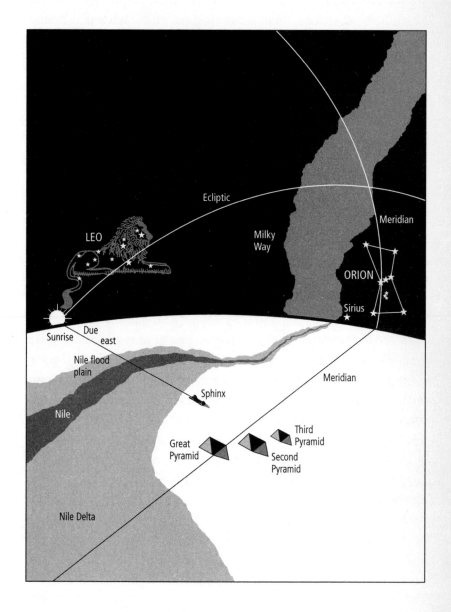

Sunrise at the vernal equinox of 10,500 BC

Artist's impression after Bauval and Hancock[2]

Any civilizations then in existence cannot have escaped the consequences – for, in the nature of things, most high civilizations develop and thrive very close to sea-level. If Plato's Atlantis was indeed one of them at the time, it must surely have been overwhelmed much as he describes. Its inhabitants must either have perished or fled in great sea-going boats to kinder, more elevated lands.

Which makes it all the more striking that several such boats – albeit from a much later era – should have been buried in great stone pits around the base of the Great Pyramid.

But there was worse. In around 10,430 BC the Earth underwent a sudden magnetic reversal,[28] the most recent of some 170 currently known to science. The precise mechanics of the process are unknown at present, as are its likely results. But within 800 years a major crustal displacement seems to have followed[11] that wiped out most of the Earth's existing animal species in the Americas, Australia and the Arctic – not least the mammoths – with a suddenness so amazing that many creatures were frozen solid before the food had even had a chance to be digested in their stomachs. At the same time the area of the Bahamas underwent a huge geological upheaval resulting in a 15 degree tilting of the local Earth's surface that is still recorded in the angles of ancient stalactites in underwater caverns on the Bahama reefs.[19]

Had Atlantis still existed in the area,[19] this must surely have finally put paid to it. And yet if there had indeed been such a displacement at the time, the Sphinx would not now be facing due east, unless it so happened that the displacement was either directly along the meridian passing through Giza or at right-angles to it.

Or unless, of course, the real date of it was rather earlier than suggested.

The imponderables, then, are still many. Yet possibly it is true that the unquiet Earth is potentially even more unquiet at certain stages in its precessional cycle. Other forces may be at work, too, such as polar imbalances caused by the slow build-up or melting of the ice-caps.

Could the witness of Giza, then, be a warning of such things – a statement that we as a species have to get all our growing and evolving done before the Last Time dawns in around AD 2450, or even before the cycle returns to its starting-point in around 15,500?

The signs are vague, the pattern of the works on the ground evidently little more than the postmark on the envelope. Somehow we need to establish with certainty who the message is addressed to. Then, in order to find out what the message is, we shall need to open the envelope and go inside.

Fortunately, that is precisely what the Great Pyramid in particular now permits us to do.

THE
EARTH
MARKER

THE GREAT PYRAMID IS POSITIVELY HUGE. The first (and the sole surviving) of the Seven Wonders of the ancient world, it remains, even today, by far the heaviest building in the world. Until the 16th century, it was also the tallest building ever built and, until the present century, the largest, too (*see Colour Plates*).

Clearly the ancients were determined that their great stone marker should not disappear or be overlooked.

However, in this case it was not the size of the blocks (as in the Valley Temple) that would ensure this, but their sheer number. At over 2.3 million blocks weighing in at an average of some $2^{1}/_{2}$ tonnes each (the heaviest weigh some 70 tonnes), the project would defy even the best-equipped of modern contractors. If, as the ancient Greek Herodotus reports, it took 100,000 workers only twenty years to complete, then they succeeded in laying them at a rate of one block every two minutes or so – even assuming that the work went on for twelve hours a day all year round.

But then Edgar Cayce (*see Chapter 1*) suggested that the job really took 100 years – and there are signs, too, that the building may have decayed and been restored at least once in remote antiquity, as Khufu's own Inventory Stela seems to hint.

And yet the precision of the engineering is amazing. Not only is the Pyramid the most accurately orientated building on Earth (its north-south axis lies within one-twelfth of a degree of true north, for example). Not only is it sited on the Earth's longest land-contact meridian, and (according to Hancock *et al*) precisely on latitude 30° *as calculated astronomically allowing for atmospheric refraction*. The lengths of its sides (all of them some 230 metres long) vary by only a few centimetres, while the ratio between its height and its base perimeter works out at just 2π – precisely that between a circle's (or a sphere's) radius and its circumference.

Not only that, but its $8^{1}/_{2}$ hectares (21 acres) of smooth casing-stones – of which only a few now survive at points around the base – were fitted together to leave *cemented* gaps of less than .05 of a centimetre (a fiftieth of an inch) in thickness, and were levelled and honed (even according to the respected, yet sceptical Flinders Petrie, the father of modern archeology) to standards of accuracy normal in modern optical work. The result was a brilliant white stone beacon that, of a midsummer noon, cast reflected beams of sunlight far across the desert *in the shape of a star*.[7,19,20] It was, in effect, a building without a shadow.

True, it would have taken a hazy day to see that reflection, or an army of observers equipped with staves to mark it out. But the effect is perfectly easy to demonstrate with the aid of a simple, polished scale-model.

'I am here,' it said. And, not content with that, it then proceeded to boggle the mind completely.

But there was more.

None other than the great Sir Isaac Newton was the first to suspect that the unit of measurement used by the building's designer was a shade over $63^{1}/_{2}$ centimetres, or 25 British inches. In fact, as more recent research has revealed, it is defined in several ways by the building itself as equalling 63.56725 centimetres, or 25.0265 British inches.[19, 20] True, conventional authorities are reluctant to accept this – especially as it turns out to be *an exact ten-millionth of*

Star-shaped reflections of the Great Pyramid's polished casing at noon of the summer solstice (contrast exaggerated)

the Earth's mean polar radius. Understandably, then, they are even less prepared to accept the corollary. For when this so-called Sacred Cubit is divided into the length of the designed base-side (which is clearly indicated by the still-surviving foundation sockets), it further turns out that there are just 365.242 of them from corner to corner – precisely the number of days, in fact, in the Earth's mean solar tropical year.

Again and again, in fact, the Pyramid announces that it stands for Planet Earth, as the details below emphasize. It is not merely that its underlying geometry is that of a sphere, or globe, rather than that of a circle (its height, after all, which corresponds to the radius, is set *at right angles* to the plane of its base perimeter, which corresponds to the circumference, so suggesting a *three-dimensional* application). Everything else fits, too.

In the diagram opposite, A, E, I and M represent the building's designed corners, as indicated by the still-surviving foundation sockets. As indicated by the inner square, however, the Pyramid was actually built (or possibly *re*built) too small – by just over 7 metres on each side – possibly in order to symbolize a Planet Earth that had yet to achieve its full potential. The theoretical shape of the full design – and thus of the building as it might eventually be realized – can nevertheless be deduced from the shape of the existing core masonry.

On the basis of the Sacred Cubit (SC) and of a 'Pyramid' or 'Primitive' Inch (P") of 2.54268 cm (1.00106 British inches) – equal to one twenty-fifth of the Sacred Cubit – this gives the extraordinary results tabulated on page 31.

The Great Pyramid, it is quite clear, stands for Planet Earth.

But if so, what do its mighty neighbours, the Second and Third Pyramids, stand for?

It does not take a genius to guess the answer.

Stunningly, they turn out to stand for our neighbouring planets Venus on the one hand and Mars, the 'red planet', on the other (see diagram page 33). Indeed, just in case there should be any doubt about it, the 'Martian' Third Pyramid was originally encased to around half its height specifically in *red granite,* as the surviving casing blocks reveal.

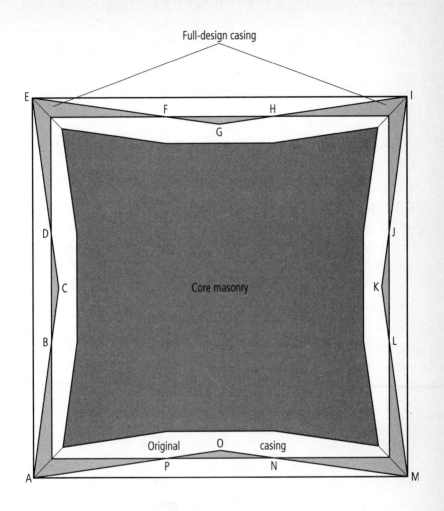

Base plan of the Great Pyramid

with concavity greatly exaggerated

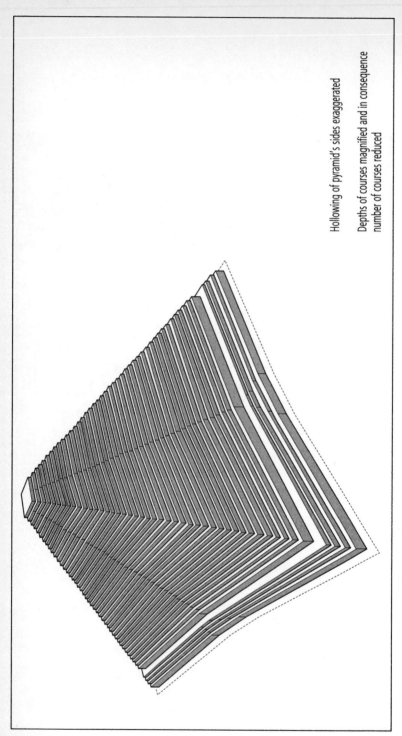

Hollowing of pyramid's sides exaggerated

Depths of courses magnified and in consequence number of courses reduced

Davidson's[7] exaggerated drawing of the Great Pyramid's concave construction

In the diagram on page 29:

AE = 365.242 SC   Number of days in Earth's mean solar tropical year (the time the sun, as seen from the Earth, takes to return to the same point in the sky)

ABDE = 365.256 SC   Number of days in Earth's sidereal year (the time the Earth takes to return to the same point in its orbit relative to the stars)

ACE = 365.259 SC   Number of days in Earth's anomalistic year (the time the Earth takes to return to the same point in its slowly revolving orbit)

AI + EM = 25,826.53 P″   Length in years of Earth's precessional cycle (the time it takes for the sun at the spring equinox to return to the same position relative to the stars as seen from the Earth – approximately)

Further figures derived from geometrical constructions based on the concavity of the sides also appear to give acceptable figures for the maximum and minimum values of the eccentricity of Earth's orbit, and for its distance from the sun.[19]

Table of the Great Pyramid's Earth correlations

Pyramid	Height	Ratio	Planet	Radius	Ratio
Great	146 metres	1	Earth	6355 km	1
Second	143.5 metres	.976	Venus	6195 km	.975
Third	66.5 metres	.452	Mars	3394 km	.531
Third (internal)	30 metres (?)	.204	Moon	1738 km	.273

Figures after (a) Lemesurier[20] / Fakhry[10] and (b) Moore[26]

Mathematical ratios between (a) pyramids and (b) planets

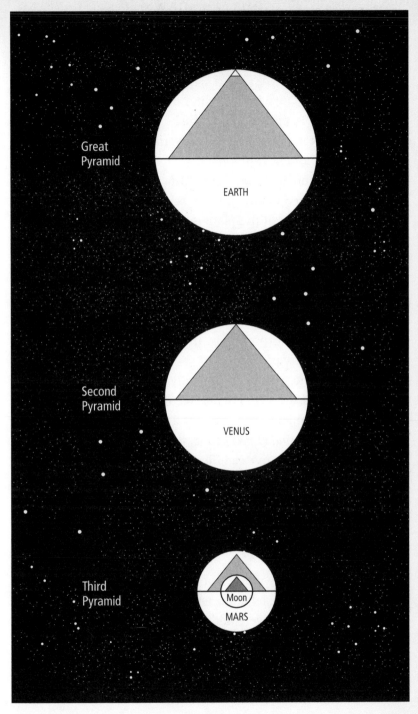

Great
Pyramid

EARTH

Second
Pyramid

VENUS

Third
Pyramid

Moon

MARS

Schematic diagram showing comparative sizes of (a) Pyramids and (b)
Planets, given that the Great Pyramid corresponds to Planet Earth

Moreover, the same Third Pyramid seems originally to have been built over a much smaller 'core pyramid' whose internal passageways still survive (*see next chapter*). This in turn may well have represented *the moon*. Once in the light, now in the darkness, this core pyramid, too, then, aptly portrays the body that it evidently represents – in this case in terms of its everlasting cycle of light and darkness, of full and new moon.

This general outcome may seem surprising. Certainly it has not been widely realized before. Yet the relative sizes of the pyramids on the one hand and of the planets on the other are so similar as virtually to rule out any other possibility. True, the proportions are not exact, as the table on page 31 reveals. Virtually spot-on in the Second Pyramid (based, once again, on the polar radius), they are much less so in the Third. But then it has long been recognized that the builders of the Second and Third Pyramids were progressively less careful and precise in their measurements than were those of their mighty predecessor.

Interestingly, too, whoever originally measured Venus seems to have had in mind the size of its visible disc rather than of its solid surface – which might suggest either a purely astronomical measurement *or an unusual respect for the 'solidity' of clouds.*

The fact might yet prove significant.

It is a sheer bonus, then, to discover that the city of which Giza was once a satellite was ancient Heliopolis, or 'Sun City' – now a part of nearby Cairo.

'Earth, satellite of Sol, care of Venus, Mars and Luna': the address on the package, then, is complete. Whoever laid out the site and raised these mighty works not only associated themselves dramatically with the constellation Orion. They left not the slightest doubt as to whom they were addressing.

It was ourselves.

And so what secrets can the inside of the package possibly hold for us?

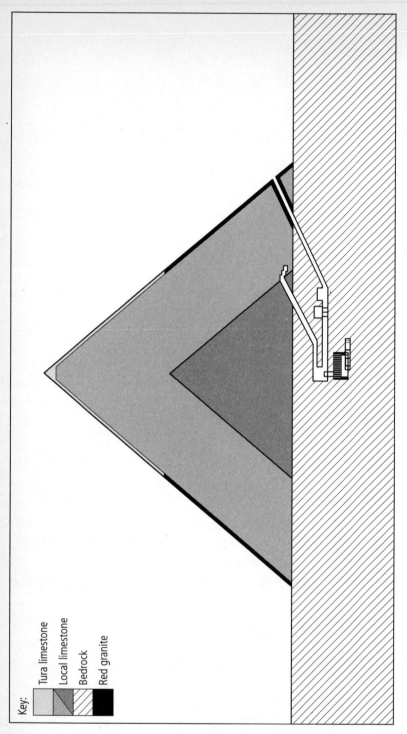

Key:

- Tura limestone
- Local limestone
- Bedrock
- Red granite

Centreline cross section through the original Third Pyramid, looking west

PARADIGMS
OF
NOTHINGNESS

THE EGYPTIAN PYRAMIDS, IT IS WELL KNOWN, for the most part contain nothing at all. Nothing, that is, beyond one or more inner chambers connected to the outside world by low, narrow passageways – and sometimes an empty stone sarcophagus.

Nearly all the pyramids boast such passageways. Normally they open from their northern sides. At Giza especially, their massed entrance shafts are trained like gun barrels on the celestial pole. But the later the pyramids' date, the more shoddy their construction. Evidently there was an original masterplan that simply became the fashion, then faded over the centuries.

And the original fashion-setters were undoubtedly the three great pyramids of Giza.

THE THIRD PYRAMID

To take these in what was almost certainly the reverse order of their construction, the Third Pyramid (normally ascribed to the pharaoh Menkure or Mycerinos) has its entrance in the middle of its north face, some 4 metres above its base and in its fifth course of masonry. A 'polar' entrance passage (lined with granite until it reaches ground level) descends some 31 metres to a stone-panelled antechamber, from which a further passage, guarded by three portcullises, leads horizontally to a more or less centrally placed subterranean chamber, in which a wooden coffin from early Christian times was once discovered. Near the top of the northern wall of this chamber, however, a further 'entrance passage' leads back north, only to stop short after a few metres. It is normally assumed that this was the entrance shaft of an original 'core pyramid', and that its extremity consequently marks the position of the latter's former northern face (*see diagram page 36*).

From the western end of the subterranean chamber, a descending ramp leads westwards to a further, granite-lined passage. From the right-hand wall of this, a descending staircase grants access to a rock-hewn chamber whose walls contain six deep niches. The passage itself, however, leads on to a large, vaulted chamber orientated north-to-south and entirely lined with red granite, its massive roof gables gouged out to form a rounded barrel vault. In this originally lay a splendid basalt sarcophagus decorated in typical Old Kingdom style. Unfortunately it was lost at sea while being looted and transported home by the British.

THE SECOND PYRAMID

Ascribed to Khafre or Chephren, the much more massive Second Pyramid has two northern entrances, both offset to the left of centre by some 13 metres. The upper one, some 11 metres above ground level, leads to the usual descending, 'polar' passage, which is lined with red granite. Once underground, this leads to a long, horizontal passage guarded by a granite portcullis.

The lower entrance, similarly offset to the left, opens up not in the building's north face, but in the ground some metres in front of it. From this, a second entrance passage slopes downwards into the bedrock, though this time at rather less than the required 'polar' angle. It leads in turn to an underground, horizontal passage guarded by a portcullis and granting access, on the right, to a subterranean, rock-cut chamber. It then leads on to a further portcullis, followed by an upward-sloping passage that joins the upper passage from below, shortly beyond where we left it.

From here, the horizontal passage leads on to a point just short of the pyramid's centre, where it enters a partially rock-hewn chamber orientated east-to-west, whose limestone roof gables project slightly above the original ground level. The tops of the north and south walls feature a pair of small, rectangular cavities, around 30 centimetres deep, that apparently correspond to the mysterious 'air shafts' of the Great Pyramid's King's Chamber (q.v. below). A pair of red squares marked on the walls some $1^{1}/_{2}$ metres below the two openings seem to mark alternative positions for them. At the chamber's far western end an empty sarcophagus of polished granite, complete with lid, is set into the floor.

THE GREAT PYRAMID

By contrast with the fairly simple passage layouts of the other two major pyramids, that of the Great Pyramid, attributed to the pharaoh Khufu or Cheops, is a positive labyrinth. This is described in full in my earlier book *The Great Pyramid Decoded*.[19]

Entered beneath a set of massive limestone gables just inside the building's north face, its familiar polar passageway once again lies to the left of centre – this time by some 7.24 metres, the precise distance by which the whole building's base-circumference appears to have been 'built small' (*see previous chapter*). Almost the whole of the passage-system is lined not with granite, but with limestone.

At a point some 12 metres down in from the entrance, however, the walls are marked by two mysterious 'scored lines', one on either side of the passage and perpendicular to its slope. After a further $17^{1}/_{2}$ metres the passage then bifurcates vertically. Its lower continuation simply continues downwards, deviating by less than

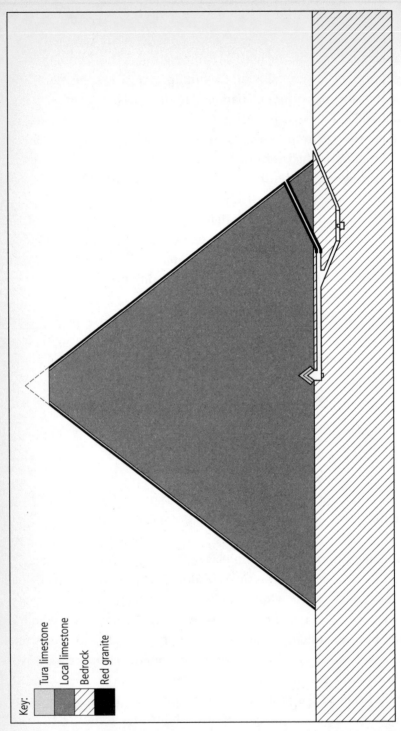

Key:

- Tura limestone
- Local limestone
- Bedrock
- Red granite

Cross section through the passageways of the Second Pyramid, looking west

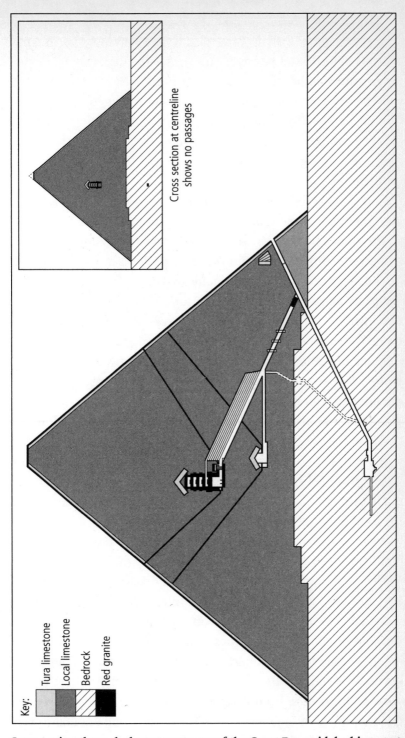

Key:
Tura limestone
Local limestone
Bedrock
Red granite

Cross section at centreline
shows no passages

Cross section through the passageways of the Great Pyramid, looking west

half a centimetre in all its 75 metres, then opens into an even more restricted horizontal passage. This passes through a crudely rock-hewn antechamber to debouch after some $8^1/2$ metres into a huge subterranean chamber that lies a good 26 metres below the ground and well beyond the centre of the pyramid whose immense bulk bears down on top of it. Orientated east to west, it contains nothing but a strangely contoured floor, a deep pit and a lot of rubble. From its far southern wall an even more restricted passageway, accessible only on hands and knees, bores a further $16^1/2$ metres into the solid rock before coming to a dead end.

The upper passageway, meanwhile, has been climbing steadily upwards through the pyramid's masonry at exactly the same angle as the entrance passage originally descended into it. Once concealed by a prismatic block of limestone, it is immediately blocked, however, by a triple granite plug that was evidently built in at the time of construction.[19] Beyond it, the passage passes through a number of stone 'collars' or 'girdles' – evidently designed to anchor the passage walls into the surrounding masonry – before opening up after nearly 38 metres into the so-called Grand Gallery. This lofty and architecturally unique corbelled hallway, built entirely on the continuing upward slope, culminates after 46 metres in a huge 'step' nearly a metre high and $1^1/2$ metres from front to back whose riser marks the exact east-west axis of the pyramid.

This marks the entrance to a low horizontal passageway that lies atop the building's 50th course of masonry and so lies exactly 153 courses below the present (and apparently designed) summit-platform. After just over a metre this leads into a strangely contoured antechamber (*see diagram overleaf*) with provision for four portcullises, one of which (of red granite) remains in place, though it is clearly a fixture, with its bottom stuck forever at roof level. Walls, roof and floor have meanwhile changed from limestone to granite, while the upper part of the chamber broadens out to well beyond the width of the passage itself. Among other things, the side walls seem to have been designed at this point to demonstrate via the quantity π and the number 365.242 (the number of days, as we have seen, in the Earth's solar tropical year) the direct mathematical links between the traditional Egyptian Royal Cubit and the pyramid's own system of measures based on Sacred Cubit and Pyramid Inch. The chamber's dimensions also relate directly to the exterior dimensions of the pyramid (*see Chapter 14*).

At the far end, the antechamber's south wall is marked by four vertical grooves, rectangular in section, that originally terminated at the bottom in what appear to have been 'scoops' and that lead up, at the top, to an anomalous section of *limestone* wall some 12 Pyramid Inches (30.51 cm) high. The former low passageway then resumes for a further $2^1/_2$ metres – making the total length of the two low sections 3.89 metres, or just over 153 Pyramid Inches (P″).

The passage now enters the magnificent King's Chamber (as it is generally known). Built entirely of red granite, its walls consist of 100 stones laid in 5 courses and its roof comprises 9 huge granite beams, all of them now cracked. Its mathematics (*see page 174*) are mind-boggling, incorporating not only the celebrated 3:4:5 triangle that is supposed to have been discovered by the much later Pythagoras, but a host of measurements based on π and the number 365.242 (once again the number of days in Earth's solar tropical year, as likewise featured in the external design).[19] It also contains an empty, lidless, granite sarcophagus that seems originally to have been positioned in the western part of the chamber exactly on the pyramid's north-south centreline.

In the chamber's north and south walls, meanwhile, are the twin entrances to what are normally referred to as 'air-shafts'. The northern one of these is rectangular in cross section (measuring about 20 cm by 13 cm) and leads upwards and northwards (carefully taking a detour to avoid the masonry of the Grand Gallery) to emerge in the 101st course of the building's original limestone casing. The southern one opens into a domed cavity reminiscent of a traditional bread oven before adopting a circular cross section (measuring about 30 cm in diameter) and heading steeply up towards the south face, where it originally emerged in the 102nd course of the casing.

And above this culminating chamber lie *five more* cavities, or mini-chambers – generally known as 'relieving' or 'construction'

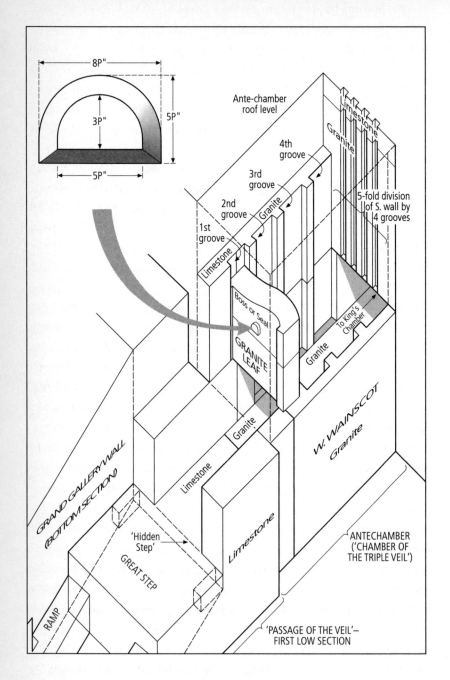

8P"

5P"

3P"

5P"

Ante-chamber
roof level

Limestone

4th
groove

Granite

3rd
groove

2nd
groove

Granite

5-fold division
of S. wall by
4 grooves

1st
groove

Limestone

Boss or Seal

To King's
Chamber

GRANITE
LEAF

Granite

W. WAINSCOT
Granite

Granite

Limestone

GRAND GALLERY WALL
(BOTTOM SECTION)

Limestone

'Hidden
Step'

ANTECHAMBER
('CHAMBER OF
THE TRIPLE VEIL')

GREAT STEP

RAMP

'PASSAGE OF THE VEIL'–
FIRST LOW SECTION

Exploded isometric projection of the Great Pyramid's antechamber

chambers – each having the same floor area as the King's Chamber below. Some 3 metres high on average, each of the bottom three of these has an irregular, rough-hewn granite floor but a flat ceiling, together with limestone east and west walls. The top two have walls entirely of limestone, while the topmost one of all is crowned not with a flat granite ceiling but with a massive limestone gable, its huge arrowhead pointing upward into the pyramid's masonry.

The King's Chamber, in effect, is merely the bottom storey of the very first tower block known to history.

But there is more. From the junction of the original ascending passage with the Grand Gallery runs a further, horizontal passage, originally concealed by a bridging slab in the floor. After nearly 39 metres this leads via a sudden downward step into the so-called Queen's Chamber. Built entirely of limestone, and with crystalline salt oozing from the walls, this gabled vault may also once have contained a sarcophagus. Many of its features have been left quite rough, but clearly distinguishable is a five-storeyed niche just over halfway along the left-hand wall, its evident displacement clearly displaying the builders' so-called Sacred Cubit. A further pair of 'air shafts' were discovered in the chamber's north and south walls in 1872 but, strangely, they had been deliberately carved to termi-nate some 13 cm (or 5 P") short of the interior of the chamber. Originally thought by Egyptologists to stop after only a few metres, they have now been shown by Rudolf Gantenbrink[1] to continue to within some 25 metres of the pyramid's north and south faces, the southern one being blocked at this point by what appears to be a small stone portcullis.

Moreover, there are two further strange features – an apparently forced passage from the top end of the Grand Gallery to the lowest of the five 'relieving chambers', and a 'well shaft' – part construct-ed, part rough-hewn and irregular – linking the junction of the Grand Gallery and the ascending passage to a point near the bottom of the descending passage, far down in the native rock below. It is not known for certain when either was made, but the evidence (*see next chapter*) certainly suggests that the 'well shaft' at least is original.

And so the mystery deepens. What were the 'forced passage' and 'well shaft' for? What could possibly lie beyond the mysterious portcullis in the Queen's Chamber's southern 'air shaft'? What secrets might the ancients still have in store for us?

And why was this extraordinarily complicated layout ever thought necessary in the first place?

—

OF
CABBAGES
AND
KINGS

—

THE EGYPTOLOGISTS HAVE AN EASY ANSWER. Either the Great Pyramid's ancient designer or his masters, they argue, were incompetents who did not know what they were about. The complications of the building's passage system, on this model, were simply the results of constant changes of plan.

As usual, in other words, the lordly beings who evidently planned and constructed the original Giza site are – for all their obvious knowledge, brilliance and advanced technology – to be dismissed as mere primitives, and not to be compared with the advanced standards of intelligence and thought that have succeeded in producing our wonderful, well-planned modern world.

No doubt the gods are laughing still.

For a start, though, it is axiomatic among the Egyptologists that the pyramids were really royal tombs. To a tome, consequently, the encyclopedias and reference books trustingly record the suggestion as if it were proven fact. The presence of sarcophagi in most of the 'burial chambers'; the traditional attribution (backed up by a variety of late inscriptions) of pyramids to particular pharaohs; the clear links with the ancient Egyptian burial rites and myths of the dead; the continuation of many of the features of the pyramids in later tombs – all this, it is argued, clearly shows that the pharaohs simply constructed them to serve as their final resting places.

A bit over the top, you have to admit – but final resting places for all that.

Unfortunately the theory does not hold water. The counter-arguments can be summed up fairly briefly:

- No pharaoh's body has ever been found in a pyramid.
- The Egyptian priesthood specifically assured the ancient Greek historian Herodotus that Khufu had not been buried in his pyramid.
- When the pyramid of Sekhemkhet at Sakkara, a few kilometres to the south of Giza, was first opened in 1954, not only were a large number of vases and some jewellery (unusually) discovered in storerooms beneath it, but the admittedly unfinished tomb chamber was found intact, complete with its alabaster sarcophagus, still sealed and inviolate, bearing the remains of a touching wreath of flowers. Amid mounting excitement, the sarcophagus was duly opened. And inside it was found…absolutely nothing.
- Many of the minor pyramids' tomb chambers are too small to have contained a body in the first place.
- There are more pyramids than pharaohs. Khufu's own father, Sneferu, is known to have built himself two at Dashur, and possibly a third at Meidum. Presumably he cannot have been buried in all three. Or was he, perhaps, as prone to change his mind as the designer of the Great Pyramid is presumed to have been? If so, those changes of mind were expensive, to say the least.
- The 18th-dynasty Queen Tetisheri had not only two tombs (another mind-changer, perhaps?), but a pyramid as well.

It might be thought that such arguments are conclusive. But no – the Egyptologists argue that if no bodies are there it is simply because

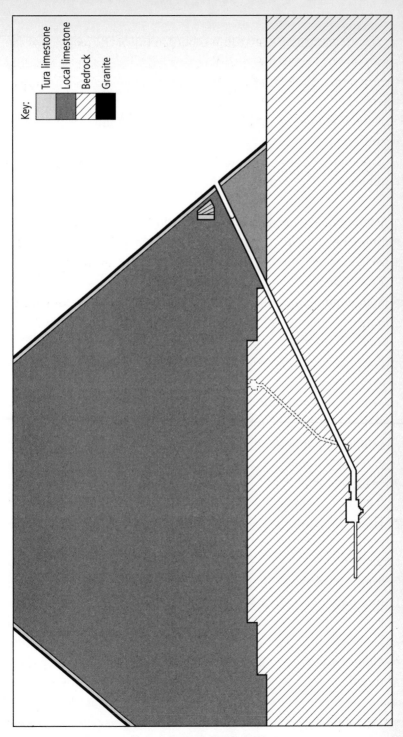

The 'change-of-mind' theory of the Great Pyramid: Plan A (see text overleaf)

they have been stolen by tomb robbers, along with whatever else the pyramids once contained. It *sounds* logical, certainly – but only if they were actually there in the first place. If you cannot point to a single example of one that was, you are on distinctly shaky ground.

It is rather like the man who claimed to be a hunter of elephants in the Arctic.

'But there *aren't* any elephants in the Arctic,' they protested.

'There you are, you see,' he replied. 'That's how good a hunter I am.'

Shaky ground doesn't worry Egyptologists, however. The pyramids – and the Great Pyramid in particular – were royal tombs, and that is that.

At which point, enter the celebrated 'change-of-mind' theory which, equally, is widely reported as though it were proven fact.

PLAN A

To start with (runs the theory) the 'royal burial' was planned to take place – logically enough, after all – deep underground. A long, sloping entrance shaft was duly sunk and a large tomb chamber begun – as it happened, well beyond the pyramid's centre (*see diagram on previous page*).

PLAN B

Before it could be finished, however, there was a change of plan. For reasons unspecified, it was now decided to move the burial upstairs to a chamber (uniquely) well above ground and approached by an ascending passage. This time it would lie directly on the pyramid's east-west axis, if somewhat to the left of its true centre. Moreover, the new chamber was to be provided with twin air shafts to north and south – though quite what the dead would want with these (especially when they hadn't been thought necessary before) has never been satisfactorily explained.

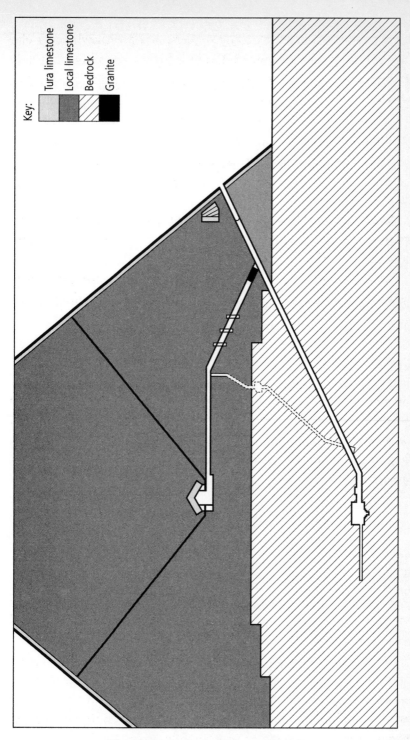

Key:
Tura limestone
Local limestone
Bedrock
Granite

The 'change-of-mind' theory: Plan B

PLAN C

Then there was yet another unexplained change of plan. The second chamber and its air shafts, too, were hurriedly left unfinished (to this extent, at least, the theory rather cleverly fits the apparent facts on the ground) and the ascending passage was extended in the form of an enormous, corbelled gallery leading still further upwards to a final, granite-lined tomb chamber based high up on the fiftieth course of masonry and approached via an antechamber of complex design. The new, ultimate tomb chamber, too, was equipped with air shafts to north and south, as well as with a built-in granite sarcophagus (it had to be built-in – it was wider than the passageways leading to it). And finally it was capped with five further chambers topped with a limestone gable, in order to protect it from the huge weight of the masonry above.

Once again, the counter-arguments are overwhelming:

- There are clear geometrical relationships between the upper and lower chambers, apparently based in the first place *on the latter*.[20,35]
- As I originally adumbrated in 1977,[19] and as Rudolf Gantenbrink has recently confirmed,[1] the northern 'air shaft' of the Queen's Chamber carefully skirts the masonry of the Grand Gallery, then continues (like its southern twin) well up past the levels of Grand Gallery and King's Chamber to very near the outer face of the pyramid. If the start of the King's Chamber project marked the abandonment of the Queen's Chamber project, all this would have been not only pointless, but needlessly expensive – since the mathematics and engineering involved are necessarily extremely sophisticated.[2] In fact, then, it is quite obvious that no such abandonment ever took place at all.
- If the Grand Gallery was necessary to plan C, it is difficult to understand why it had been unnecessary to plans A or B.
- There exists to this day in the rock 100 metres to the east of the Great Pyramid a set of workings known as the 'trial passages', known for the most part only to pyramid specialists.

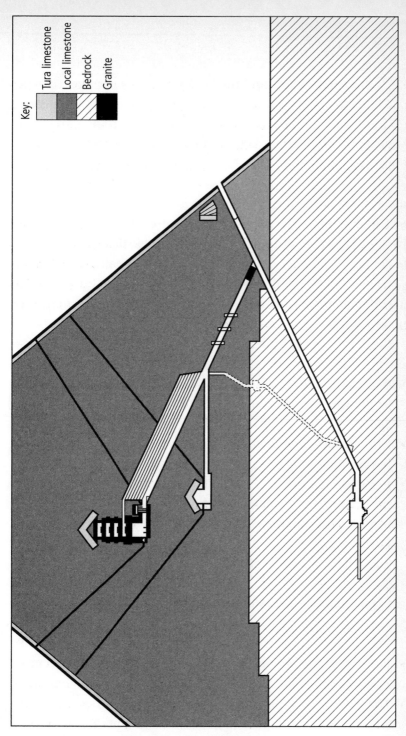

The 'change-of-mind' theory: Plan C

Apparently sunk as a kind of prototype before work on the pyramid began, they contain sections of *all* the main passageways (apart from the King's Chamber passage) to their correct lateral dimensions, if with some differences. This argues that a coherent plan existed at the outset, even though some of its details were either imperfectly understood or still fluid at the time.

Once again, however, the Egyptologists remain unconvinced – as well they might, given the difficulty of explaining the complete passage-layout in terms of the familiar tombic theory.

Yet, as we have seen, the tombic theory is really a non-starter. Consequently the difficulty disappears. The passageways, it seems, are simply as they are. And so what is needed is not a new interpretation of the old theory, but a new theory entirely.

But where does this leave the pharaohs whose names are associated with the pyramids? Where does it leave the ancient Egyptian myths and funeral rites?

In the case of the pharaohs, the Inventory Stela (*see Chapter 1*) already suggests an answer. Far from building the great pyramids of Giza, the pharaohs seem merely to have appropriated – and possibly restored – structures that were already there.

In the case of the myths and funeral rites, an even more earth-shaking conclusion emerges. It is not, after all, that the pyramids were based on the myths and rites: *instead, the myths and rites were based on the pyramids.*

The whole structure of Egyptian religion, in short – and especially its tall tales of sky gods and lordly bringers of civilization – derived from the knowledge enshrined in those mighty monuments. Possibly it was based, too, on distant, misty folk-memories of the ancient founders themselves. Osiris and Isis, Horus and Set went back to real originals in the Dream Time, to real precursors during the precessional First Time of the eleventh millennium BC. Even today, in fact, many of the world's great religions continue to echo those Osirian symbolisms of remote antiquity as they try to put us back in touch with the ancient gods of the beginning.

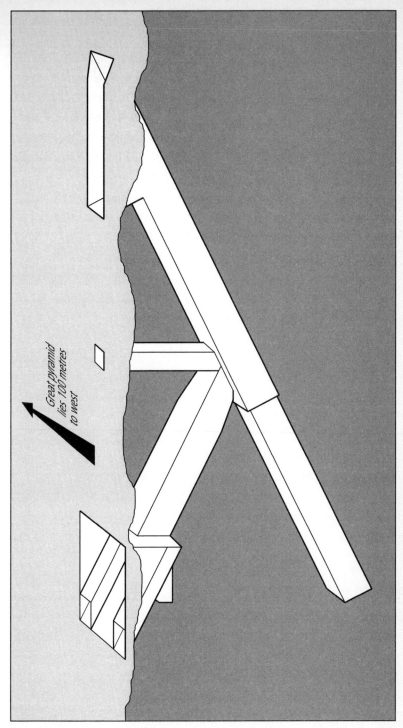

Great pyramid lies 100 metres to west

The Trial Passages display sections of almost all the main passageways
including a differently-positioned 'well shaft' and a sloping subterranean passage

But what if that re-encounter is really a much more practical, blood-and-guts affair? What if it involves actually reading the message that the founders left for us in enduring stone, there amid the sands of Giza? What if it then involves responding to it in the most practical and physical of ways?

If so, then we finally have to solve the riddle of what the passageways mean.

7

PATHS
OF
LIFE

ROYAL TOMB; PHARAONIC CENOTAPH; TREASURE HOUSE; Atlantean time capsule; biblical storehouse; theodolite; astronomical observatory; weights-and-measures standard; cosmic powerhouse; meditation centre; temple of initiation; irrigation pump for the Nile delta. All of these and more have been proposed as theories to explain the Great Pyramid and its internal passage system – and none of them holds water.

Not even the irrigation pump.

Were the theorists to be let loose on the Second and Third Pyramids, too, no doubt their functions would turn out to be just as bewilderingly diverse.

It is all rather like reading preconceived conclusions into the Bible, or Nostradamus, or any other complex text. *Taken out of context*, almost any verse can be taken to mean almost anything. Nostradamus, for example, can be (and has been) made to predict everything from the deaths of the Kennedys and the future 'nuking' of New York to the lives of mere showbiz personalities such as Sean Connery and Michelle Pfeiffer.

To say nothing of Armageddon itself.

Once you have decided that the Bible, similarly, is really a thesis on (say) constipation and its cure, passages such as Exodus 34:4 are a gift. *And Moses rose up early in the morning*, it reads (give or take a word or two), *went up into the mountain...and took two tablets...*

It is on exegetics of only slightly greater respectability that biblical fanatics and Nostradamian commentators alike thrive and prosper.

In the case of the pyramids, too, you tend to see in them what you are looking for. They are, in a sense, mirrors of the soul. To this extent they can, of course, be useful. But then, so can a busy telephone box when it is raining, or a mobile phone when you need a hammer.

Needless to say, though, to use them in this way is to wilfully squander valuable resources. Both telephone box and mobile phone are much better used in their proper context.

Much the same goes for the pyramids, too. They need to be interpreted *in their proper context*. To do otherwise is merely to ape on a different level the unthinking visitors who insist on using the coffer in the King's Chamber of the Great Pyramid as a urinal.

To say nothing of the telephone box.

We have already established, after all, that the Great Pyramid stands for nothing less than Planet Earth. The Second Pyramid, similarly, stands for Venus. The originally red-clad Third Pyramid stands for Mars, while its inner core pyramid seems to represent the moon. Any passages through the pyramids *have therefore to be seen as passages through the respective planets*.

The Great Pyramid's passageways are passages through Earth. The Second Pyramid's passageways are passages through Venus. The Third Pyramid's passageways are passages through Mars and moon. Designed by who knows whom, but passages none the less.

Yet what is it that can undertake such passages through their respective planetary environments? Surely, only life itself.

And so the passages turn out to be *passages of life*. They are pathways for living beings to tread – be they lowly or extremely advanced. And what befalls them there is what is destined to befall life itself on the three planets in question.

The suggestion may seem fantastic. Yet, as we shall go on to see, the evidence of the Great Pyramid in particular is quite specific on this point. The fact should give us pause for thought – for it has potentially mind-boggling implications.

THE PASSAGES THROUGH MARS AND MOON

The Third Pyramid's passageways, on this basis, cannot help but represent life on Mars and the moon. Interpreted literally, their layout in side elevation suggests that, in the first instance, any such life has to come *from outside*. The entrance passages of both outer and 'core' pyramids, after all, lie 'up in the air' – a little way up on their respective north faces, that is. Indeed, they point directly at the celestial pole.

Can it be, then, that life is envisaged as descending on the two bodies *from a planet orbiting one of the immediate circumpolar stars* – possibly one of the succession of Pole Stars itself? Or should we be thinking in rather more general terms of an unspecified extraplanetary and possibly even intercosmic origin?

Certainly extraplanetary seeding is not as way-out an idea as it may at first seem. It has long been proposed, for example, by the eminent British astronomer Fred Hoyle. On this model, space would be seen not as the kind of sterile graveyard that it is often supposed to be, but as positively brimming with potential life that is only waiting to descend on whatever planetary bodies offer suitable conditions for it to develop and flourish, much as happens on Earth thanks to the tiny seeds, bacteria and fungi that throng the swirling atmosphere. All the molecular building-blocks of life, in fact, are known to be out there.

But then another possible explanation offers itself, too. Perhaps the passageways represent the ingress of alien life-forms *from Earth* – the establishment, in other words, of future human space colonies designed as self-supporting research-stations and, in the case of the moon, as low-gravity jumping-off stations for the planets and beyond?

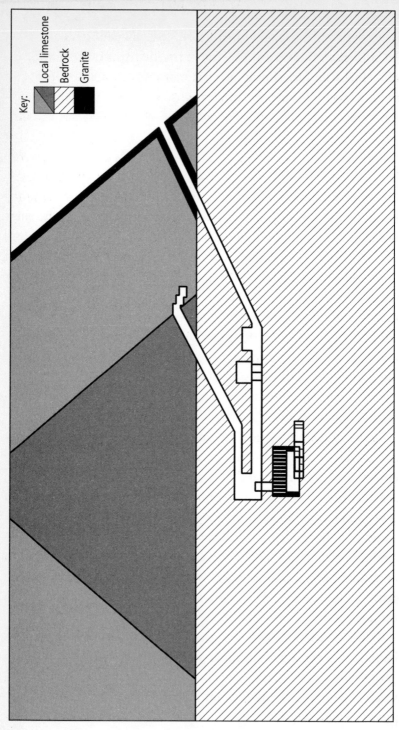

The passage system of the Third Pyramid, looking west

Either way, the message of the Third Pyramid is not encouraging. On both planets the initiative leads first downwards, then horizontally, finally terminating in a common 'tomb chamber'. There is, in other words, a pronounced decline, followed by a period of relative stasis – but ultimately no way out. On both bodies the outcome is ultimately the same.

From the original common 'tomb chamber', of course, a ramp does lead downwards and westwards to another chamber even further underground. Whether this is part of the original plan may be doubted. Certainly the Egyptologists see it as a later development, no doubt connected with the remodelling of the original core structure to its larger design. Bearing in mind the evident inaccuracy of scale in this latter (if the planetary hypothesis advanced in Chapter 4 is valid), we may well conclude that the original parameters drawn up by the ancient founding fathers were by this time starting to be fudged, modified and even ignored. The fact, though, that the upper part of the planned red outer casing was, in the event, to be finally completed in less expensive white limestone may (as we shall see) be due to a much more intriguing possibility altogether…

At all events, the splendid western tomb chamber and its associated granite-hewn vault may merely have been later modifications to suit the whim of the pharaoh Menkure and his family, who clearly regarded the monument as his. Certainly, elements of the same design crop up in their own funereal architecture.

Just assuming, however, that the design is as originally envisaged, then the message is perhaps quite literally that on both planetary bodies life is likely eventually to be forced underground – presumably by ever harsher conditions experienced on the surface.

Thanks to the moon's low gravity, certainly, virtually any atmosphere that it once had has long since gone. Surface temperatures consequently range from 105°C by day to –105°C at night – each of which lasts all of an Earth fortnight. Only deep underground, consequently, could any unprotected water-based life possibly now survive – and life as we know it is very much water- and carbon-based.

Otherwise the moon is a dead world.

Much the same applies to Mars. It has an atmosphere, it is true, but this now consists mainly of carbon dioxide and has a pressure over a hundred times less than that on Earth. Thanks to its relatively low gravity, the planet's gaseous envelope has been steadily leaching into space for millions of years. Thus, carbon- and water-based life could once have existed here – but its continued survival into our own times must depend on its having long since retreated far underground.

The message of the Third Pyramid, then, seems to fit the *historical* case on various counts. But does it also fit the possible future one? Could it be suggesting that the space colonies of the future, too, will have only limited success and never develop any autonomous existence of their own? Could it be presaging an ultimate retreat into the interior?

If so, then the granite lining of the further passage and the impressive and clearly deliberately rounded barrel-vaulting of the equally granite-lined western chamber may suggest, in terms of the code suggested in Chapter 10 below, that an independent high technology with space implications will in due course be developed by the colonies on both planets – as, indeed, seems to follow from their likely function as research stations. Yet they themselves will still have no independent posterity of their own.

Their future is still a dead end. Their world is still ultimately a tomb.

This accords entirely with the physical facts of the case. The moon's surface gravity is only one-sixth of Earth's, Mars's a little less than half. Born and raised in such comparatively weightless environments, the descendants of the first colonists will have lunar or Martian bones, lunar or Martian musculatures, lunar or Martian cardiovascular systems. Consequently the lunar colonists especially will be for ever *physically incapable* of returning to Earth. However harsh and life-threatening their environments may become, they will have virtually nowhere else to go. Unable to adjust back to terrestrial gravity or its equivalent, they will be condemned to live for ever on low-gravity worlds that will in all probability offer conditions no more propitious for their ultimate survival than those on Mars or the moon.

Both planets, in short, represent evolutionary dead ends.

On the whole, then, the interpretation of the Third Pyramid's passageways as a vision of the Martian and lunar future seems highly apt – even more so than a view of them as depictions of ancient planetary history.

THE PASSAGES THROUGH VENUS

Inevitably, then, the passage system of the Second Pyramid, seen in side elevation, has in its turn to represent life on Venus. Here, though, there seems to be no possible question of a reference to events in the distant past. Venus seems always to have been profoundly hostile to life. It has a surface temperature of nearly 500°C and an atmosphere consisting largely of carbon dioxide with an admixture (at upper levels, at least) of sulphuric acid.

The passageways of the Second Pyramid, then, can only refer to *future* life on Venus – a Venus that has by then presumably been transformed by terraforming into a habitable planet. The idea is no mere fantasy. Plans are already afoot (courtesy of the late Carl Sagan, among others) to bombard its atmosphere with chemicals and/or seed it with green algae and carefully engineered bacteria. Decades of long rains could conceivably be induced, the atmosphere transformed, ever higher forms of terrestrial life introduced. We could become founding gods on our own account.

And the whole process could take only a few hundred years.

But then what? Once again, the message of the Second Pyramid is not encouraging. In fact it is even more depressing than that of its smaller neighbour. Evidently seeded, once again, from space, and supported (as the entrance passage's granite lining suggests) by an advanced technology wielded by higher intelligence (in this case presumably our own), it is destined for a steady decline, a long period of stasis – albeit this time at or near the surface – and then oblivion.

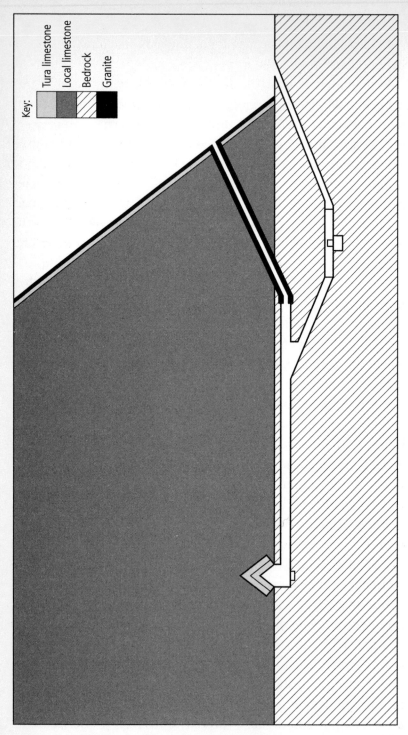

Key:

Tura limestone
Local limestone
Bedrock
Granite

The Second Pyramid's passage system, looking west

No less, in fact, than has frequently befallen remote colonies here on Earth in the past.

Perhaps, in this case, the decline and extinction occurs because the colonial culture never succeeds in achieving the total harmony with the planet that would be signified by its arrival at the building's centre. True, it does just about manage to get its head above water during the evidently aspirational era signified by the central chamber with its upward-pointing gable, but despite at least one 'booster injection' from outside (apparently signified by the portcullis in the entrance passage, as per the Great Pyramid's code below) it remains for ever off-centre, lacking some vital ingredient, insufficiently adapted to survive.

Possibly the planetary environment will prove just too difficult to control.

Curiously enough, however, there is a completely unexpected parallel development, signified by the lower entrance at ground level. During the course of the great experiment, it seems, *Venusian life somehow manages to develop on its own.* Possibly it is triggered by the induced atmospheric changes. Possibly it was always there in germ. But at some stage it comes into being – albeit apparently of a much lower order, or even literally underground – and is even given periodic advanced support from outside. Yet eventually it is destined to share the same miserable fate as the colonists and their menagerie of imported life-forms.

Death. Extinction. Oblivion.

True, there are signs of an attempted 'break-out' during the Final Era – which possibly coincides with the Final Era likewise seemingly depicted in the Great Pyramid for Planet Earth itself (*see next chapter*). Possibly it takes the form of a would-be return to the home planet, symbolized by the dummy 'air shafts' of the central chamber with its upward-pointing gable. Indeed, there are apparently two such initiatives – the one merely planned, the other, at a higher level, actually acted upon. But both have in the end to be abandoned. As the sunken, lidded 'tomb' suggests, the colonists are destined to subside in the end into foreign, Venusian earth.

Ashes to new ashes, dust to new dust.

The colonists, it seems, can no longer obtain vital help and support from Earth – and possibly they are not now welcome back at home, either. There may be good reasons for this. For a start, they are by now almost certainly far too numerous to make the homeward journey. Moreover, if – as seems likely from the similarities in 'tomb chamber' design – the Martian and Venusian Final Eras do indeed correspond to that predicted for Earth itself in the Great Pyramid (see below), then the signs are that terrestrial humanity may only recently have undergone a planetary catastrophe of its own, and that its more advanced survivors are even now headed far out towards the stars...

In short, there is nobody at home. The space colonies must fend for themselves.

Such, it seems, is the message of the 'Venusian' Second Pyramid, bequeathed to us by some intelligence as yet unknown. But again and again one nagging question keeps surfacing: 'When is all this to be?'

Already we seem to have established that the developments indicated are more likely to be for our future than for our past. To that extent, there is a distinct prophetic element in the respective pyramids' messages.

As we shall go on to see, in fact, there is clear evidence at Giza of a prophetic technology of a very high order indeed, based on who knows what linkages between the planets and the cosmos through which they are whirling.

Yet nowhere in the Second or Third Pyramids does either the era or the timescale seem to be specified. Possibly this is merely because we have not yet looked. Somewhere within both pyramids there may be some marker – possibly astronomical – indicating a starting point. Somewhere, equally, there may be some indication of temporal scale.

Just as, in the event, there appear to be in the Great Pyramid itself...

8

THE
PASSAGES
THROUGH
EARTH

SEEN IN SIDE-ELEVATION, THE PASSAGES of the Great Pyramid present a much more complicated picture than those of either of its two neighbours. We have already seen that this is evidently deliberate, not accidental. The resulting pattern bears witness, not to woolly-minded changes of plan, but to a complex destiny for life on Planet Earth.

And that destiny is evidently our own.

For over a century now, indeed, the more open-minded of investigators have realized that the overall pattern of the passageways is stunningly reminiscent of human history itself.

It was in 1865, in fact, that a young Scottish shipbuilder by the name of Robert Menzies first came up with the idea that it could represent a prophetic blueprint for humanity itself. True, he also proposed that the blueprint had been laid down by none other than the Deity – a tradition that is perhaps understandable in terms of contemporary beliefs and enthusiasms, and that still dies hard even today.

Nevertheless, the theory is an attractive one.

The nexus of the whole design, after all, (*see diagram opposite*) is clearly the junction between the ascending passage, the great, corbelled Grand Gallery, the horizontal Queen's Chamber passage and the so-called 'well shaft'. Compare this with the corresponding nexus in world history that is the BC/AD divide, and it becomes clear that the ascending passage itself could correspond to the founding eras of Sumer, Babylon, Assyria, Persia, Greece and Rome – to say nothing of those of Hinduism, Buddhism, Shinto, Confucianism, Taoism and Judaism. Or possibly it refers only to these latter, 'higher' developments, while the steady decline in values that various aspects of the former civilizations also represented is reflected in the corresponding section of the *descending* passage far below.

Either the Grand Gallery or the Queen's Chamber passage would then represent the world of Christianity and Islam, of Renaissance and Reformation ideals, of the Age of Enlightenment and Industrial Revolution, and eventually of modern science and technology. And the still-descending entrance passage, as it debouches into the ghastly subterranean chamber with its bottomless pit and its eventual dead end passage would refer to the continual decline in values and disintegration of society and its ideals that seems to have played counterpoint to these various more hopeful developments.

Actually, the divide is more or less inevitable. Dark and light, good and evil are always functions of each other.[18] The bifurcation of history as apparently depicted in the Great Pyramid is merely duality writ large upon the stage of time.

Meanwhile the upper passageways have culminated in the extraordinary King's Chamber complex, with its antechamber, its portcullises, its death-defying 'tomb chamber' and the latter's five further superincumbent chambers crowned with their upward-pointing gable – all apparently depicting not only our present, but our potential future. And from this, two 'air shafts' apparently indicating some kind of final escape from Earth...

Such, then, were some of the features noticed by Menzies. The whole thing was a gift to the religious. There in solid stone, in effect,

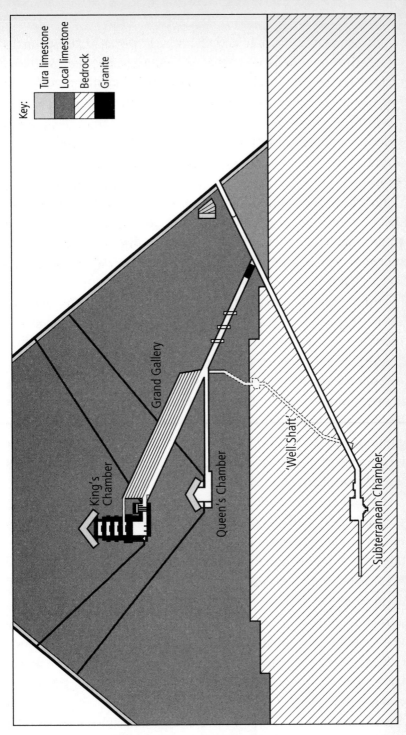

Broad overview of the Great Pyramid's passage system

was the Bible itself. The Old Testament era, the New Testament era, the promise of the eventual Millennium or Kingdom of Heaven on Earth – even, in the 'well shaft', the redemptive mission of Christ to the unredeemed in the lower passageways. But then, as we have already suggested, such notions and their even more ancient precursors may themselves have derived, at least in part, from the Great Pyramid itself and those ancient lords of Giza who designed it...

Yet even this religious attitude to the building and its message had its value. Starting with the then Astronomer Royal for Scotland, Charles Piazzi Smyth,[31] the idea was developed, re-worked, extended, published and re-published almost *ad infinitum*. Pyramidology became a field of study in its own right, only much later to become regarded as a discredited fad that had had its day. The ideas of Pyramidologists such as David Davidson[7] became national headlines – especially for the British, who by this time had somehow got hold of the extraordinary idea that they and their Empire had some divinely-appointed part to play in the culminating stages of the process. British Israelites and Jehovah's Witnesses alike drew huge inspiration from the proposition.

The number of books on the subject grew and grew. Soon the sceptics were suggesting that, piled one upon the other, they would make a pyramid even larger than the original.

At least there was one positive result, however. The idea survived. Consequently it was still there in 1977 when I published my first book on the subject, which was based largely on the Pyramidologists' ideas.[19] It was still there, too, in 1987, when I published my second, which was based far more on my own.[20] It was still there in 1994, when Robert Bauval and Adrian Gilbert (who, as a sales representative for Element Books, was familiar with my work) published their hugely influential breakthrough book *The Orion Mystery*.[1] It was still there, consequently, in 1995, when Graham Hancock (who was similarly familiar with my ideas) published his bestselling and equally influential *Fingerprints of the Gods*.[13] And it was still there in 1996, when Bauval and Hancock finally got together to publish their impressive *Keeper of Genesis*.[2]

It had been a long process of continual resumé and review, leading eventually to a more dynamic one of thesis and antithesis. On the one hand, the approach 'from inside', concentrating on the Great Pyramid's passage system. On the other, that 'from outside', concentrating on the external site data.

But in terms of Hegelian dialectics, thesis and antithesis inevitably combine in the end to produce a higher synthesis which in turn goes on to provide a new thesis in its own right. The two sides of the arch are finally cemented and made firm by the culminating capstone – even though this merely goes on to provide the foundation for one side of a new arch altogether...

Such, it may be, is the role of the present volume.

The Pyramidologists, then, had done their work. The inside of the Pyramid had been surveyed *ad nauseam*, its measurements refined by an unending stream of astronomers, surveyors, mathematicians, engineers and plain, enthusiastic amateurs. And the more they looked, the more the facts fitted the theory.

True, the phenomenon is a familiar enough one. Researchers with new theories to prove continually find new evidence to back them up. The evidence grows, develops, becomes more and more complex. Eventually it becomes far *too* complex and collapses under its own weight. Whereupon a new theory has to be proposed to fit the newly accumulated evidence – and the process starts all over again.

It happened with Ptolemy and Copernicus. It happened with the Bible and Darwin. It happened with Ussher and Lyell. It happened with Newton and Einstein. No doubt, too, it will happen with the expanding universe and the associated Big Bang – and eventually, perhaps, with Einstein himself...

Possibly all this says something significant about the relationship between human consciousness and perceived reality.

Yet often elements of the old theory survive the process. They become not more and more difficult to sustain, but increasingly simple and obvious. This is always the sign of a good hypothesis. And, in the event, it is exactly what has happened in the case of the Pyramidologists. It is precisely thanks to the untiring efforts of researchers such as Adam Rutherford[35] that the measurements of the Great Pyramid's passage-system are now known to an extraordinary degree of accuracy. Indeed, his figures may be regarded as definitive.

Consequently we can now read the design entirely for what it says, rather than for what we might like it to say – whether about the Bible, Christianity or anything else. And it turns out that the Great Pyramid's passage system is indeed a blueprint. Not Divinely ordained, perhaps, but certainly designed by some advanced intelligence.

As Arthur C. Clarke's perceptive Third Law puts it: *Any sufficiently advanced technology is indistinguishable from magic.*[4]

And so we can now start to put more flesh on the bones. The descending passage does indeed represent a decline in terrestrial affairs from what appears to be not merely some former state of grace, but an actual celestial origin (life on Earth, in other words, was itself originally seeded *from elsewhere*) – a decline leading eventually to an era of 'hell on earth'. From this there is admittedly an eventual escape (the dead-end passage) – but it is one that (to quote Thomas Hobbes's memorable phrase) is nasty, brutish and short.

From some point during the long decline, however, a new, more hopeful, 'upward' initiative (the ascending passage) emerges, eventually to burst forth into intense life and a higher, more exalted dimension (the Grand Gallery) at what appears to be the nexus point of terrestrial history (the Pyramidologists, inevitably, associate this with the Crucifixion). Much later on, this initiative reaches its culmination with the attainment of a level that seems to be one of intense preparation and even transformation. A series of strange encounters (in the antechamber) then leads on into a final chamber (the King's Chamber) whose open, empty tomb speaks of the transcending of death – i.e. either individual immortality or sheer racial survival. This evidently involves some kind of ultimate escape either from physical existence or from Earth itself, and access is thereby gained to a series of five even higher levels of consciousness and/or existence.

At a lower level, meanwhile, an alternative and much less excit-ing path of eventual transcendence (the Queen's Chamber com-plex) still remains to be opened. There are signs that this will have to be done by sheer, patient effort. Success may be heavily depen-dent on the first wave's attainment of the five higher levels just mentioned. Only then will any help from above manifest itself and a belated escape from physicality – or from Earth itself – at last be-come available. Even for those on the lowest path of all, indeed, transfer to either of the higher routes remains possible (via the 'well shaft') provided that a certain minimum level of develop-ment is maintained.

Such, then, is a superficial reading of the Great Pyramid's passage-system. But how does this relate to the recently-established facts on the ground? To what extent does what goes for Giza go for Planet Earth itself? Here much depends on the discovery within the pyramid of a timescale and a definite starting point.

As it happens, these have long since been unearthed...

9

THE CHRONOGRAPH

ONE OF THE MOST OBVIOUS WAYS TO DEFINE a building and its contents in time – particularly across such vast vistas of time as are evidently in play at Giza – is to use astronomy. An inscription, after all, can decay and become illegible. All knowledge of its characters and language can disappear.

But the stars remain forever.

Now one thing in particular has always been known about the stars. They are reliable timekeepers. Used since the most ancient times to tell the time of night, they also tell the season of the year. And not only of the common terrestrial year, but of the mighty, precessional Great Year, too.

Thanks to the spinning Earth's angle of tilt (some $23^{1}/_{2}°$) and its slow, gyroscopic wobble (whose cycle lasts some 26,000 years), all kinds of phenomena result. The vernal sun appears successively in sign after zodiacal sign, so producing the slow procession of astrological ages, each of which lasts some 2,150 years. Thus, the year 10,531 BC (or thereabouts) marked the onset of the Age of Leo (compare Chapter 2 above). 4,080 BC saw the beginning of the age of Taurus, 1930 BC that of Aries. Currently passing through the

75

latter stages of the ensuing Age of Pisces, we shall go on to enter that of Aquarius in AD 2371 – a good deal later, it has to be said, than either the stage musical or most 'New Age' writers would have us believe. Whether this so-called 'precession of the equinoxes' has any of the deep, esoteric effects on us that the latter claim is at best debatable, though it does seem, among other things, to be at least one of the causes of the ice ages through which Earth appears to pass at long intervals.

But there are other effects, too. The band within which the sun, the planets and the constellations of the zodiac revolve (known as the ecliptic), slowly moves (for any given date in the year) first higher, then lower in the sky in a cycle that similarly lasts some 26,000 years. True, this happens annually, too, as far as the night sky is concerned – once again because of the planet's tilt. The sun, self-evidently, is higher in the sky in summer than in winter. But the annual cycle is of no use for dating purposes over the periods evidently envisaged here. The precessional cycle, by contrast, is ideal.

Which is no doubt why the ancient lords of Giza evidently resorted to it in order to establish their eternal fix in time.

Obtaining any kind of fix, whether astronomically in time or geographically in space, involves the taking of bearings. As anybody who has ever navigated a boat by traditional methods will know, a single bearing merely produces a position-line, and one's craft could be at any point along it. A second bearing at a fairly wide angle to the first, however, narrows down the possibilities considerably. The point where the two position-lines cross could well turn out to be exactly where one currently is. However, errors and inaccuracies are always possible, and so a third bearing is advisable. The three resulting position-lines will now form a 'triangle of probability', and the true position is likely to lie somewhere within it.

Much the same applies to astronomical fixes in space – except that the addition in this case of a third dimension makes it essential to obtain not only a third fix, but preferably a fourth and fifth as well.

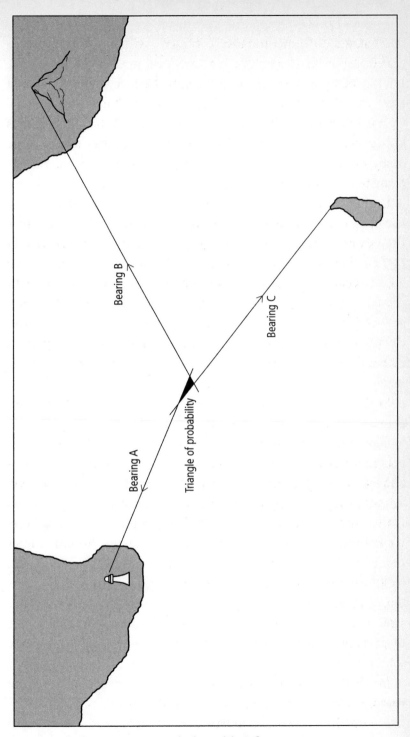

A typical maritime fix

Astronomical *time* fixes, however, are a different matter. Theoretically, a single bearing might be sufficient, provided that the identity of the star in question is known. However, in the case of the Giza project that identity inevitably had to remain an enigma, since neither the chosen star's name nor the script in which it was written could be relied upon to survive the passing of the ages. Some kind of graphic description might have helped, but such a description would inevitably have fitted millions of other stars, too.

And so, in practice, the nautical (or astronautical) technique of fixes based on multiple bearings would once again have had to be brought into play.

One of the recent triumphs of Bauval *et al* has been to show that the Great Pyramid does indeed incorporate such a fix – a fix determined by the building's four so-called 'air shafts'.

These enigmatic features not only seem to symbolize channels of escape and/or ingress. Aimed precisely north-and-south, they also serve as perpetual astrolabes – and not just as any old astrolabes, either, but as sighting devices of truly laser-like precision. Hence, presumably, the infinite care with which the builders chased them through the building's succeeding courses of masonry, almost as though their lives depended on it.

The precise orientation of the air shafts was obviously regarded as absolutely vital. They were the means whereby the whole, mighty structure was to be anchored to the stars.

Using sophisticated modern computer programmes, Bauval and his colleagues have succeeded in identifying the particular stars that were targeted as they passed successively through the north-south meridian – or 'culminated', to use the astronomical jargon. The northern shaft from the King's Chamber was aimed fairly and squarely at Alpha Draconis; the corresponding shaft from the Queen's Chamber at Beta Ursae Minoris, in the Little Bear. The southern shaft from the Queen's Chamber pinpointed Sirius, the Dog Star, while that from the King's Chamber was trained precisely on Zeta Orionis.

Several points demand to be made at this juncture. The first is that Alpha Draconis, chief star of the Dragon, is one of a succession

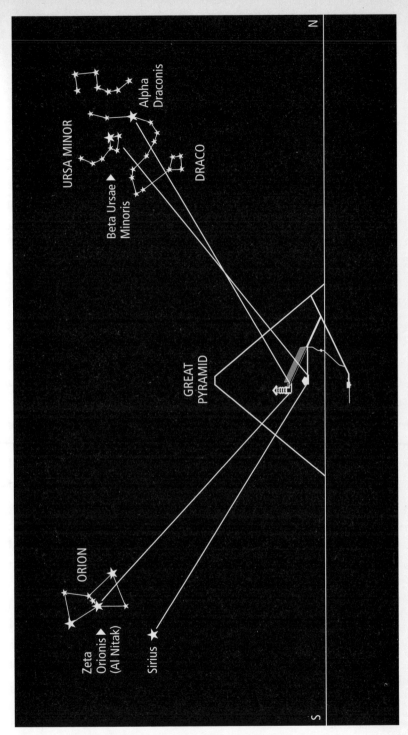

Stellar alignments of the Great Pyramid's 'air-shafts'

after Bauval and Gilbert [1]

of stars that serve as Pole Star to succeeding ages. None of these ever lies exactly at the celestial pole, however – not Alpha Draconis, not Vega, not even the present Polaris (Alpha Ursae Minoris). As the ages precess, so do the circumpolar stars revolve and sway, successively bringing now one star, now another closest to the centre. Polaris only became the Pole Star in quite recent times. Vega was the Pole Star of around 14,000 BC and, barring catastrophic polar shifts, will be again in around 10,000 years from now. *But Alpha Draconis was the Pole Star specifically of the third millennium BC.*

The second point is that Sirius (Alpha Canis Majoris) was regarded by the ancient Egyptians as having enormous importance, embodying as it did the goddess Isis herself, and timing as it also did the whole agricultural calendar by its heliacal rising (i.e. its rising with the sun). The tradition dated from at least the third millennium BC. It was entirely appropriate, then, that the shaft targeting it should emerge (or rather nearly emerge – for its ends were originally blocked) from what is known as the *Queen's* Chamber.

The traditional names, it seems, may possibly preserve a vague memory of the original true associations.

The third point is that Zeta Orionis is the left-hand star of Orion's belt – i.e. none other than Al Nitak, *the selfsame star that the Great Pyramid itself clearly symbolizes on the Giza star map.* Orion, then, equally appropriately, is directly associated not only with the pyramid itself, but specifically with the extraordinary King's Chamber initiative and whatever it eventually represents.

But *when* would all these correlations apply?

The computers revealed that there was only one possible time in all the years since the presumed inception of the great Giza project in around 10,500 BC. *That date was 2,500 BC,* give or take a few years.

True, as the constellations gradually rise and fall in the night sky, that time will come again. On present estimates, it will take another 6,000 years or so. But the most reasonable assumption has to be that the designer was setting his astronomical clock for the *next* time the pattern occurred. The particular epoch pinpointed, in other words, was the third millennium BC. That was when the message of the inner passageways was to be activated. Strung like some invisible spider's web between the stars, the great astronomical fix was merely awaiting the arrival of the unknowing flying insect that was its chosen time.

And then the trap would be sprung.

Even so, the date is not precise. Surveyors and engineers, after all, have long reported that the centre of the Pyramid has subsided by some 30 centimetres over the centuries.[35] As a result, most of the above-ground passages and shafts have become slightly steeper than they were originally. It is not clear that Bauval *et al* have taken account of this in their calculations. In which case, the upshot would be that the northern shafts originally targeted slightly more northerly stars than those suggested, while the southern shafts targeted Sirius and Al Nitak rather earlier than suggested – possibly nearer 2,600 BC than 2,500 BC. This would still be perfectly satisfactory, though, given that it is the date more normally assigned to the Pyramid by Egyptologists, as well as the date apparently pinpointed (as we shall see) by the entrance to the passageways themselves.

But then absolute precision is in any case not of the essence here. It seems likely that the 'air shaft' time fix is merely designed to pinpoint a particular *era*. Might there not, then, be some even more specific dating indicated within the passageways?

Much the same question seems to have occurred to Professor Charles Piazzi Smyth back in 1864. In fact his former boss at the Cape of Good Hope observatory, the renowned astronomer Sir John Herschel, had already been working on the problem. The descending passage, he had established as long ago as the late 1830s, had pointed (like the northern shaft of the King's Chamber) directly at Alpha Draconis during the third millennium BC, but in this case during the period of its *lower* culmination – i.e. when it was transiting the *reverse* meridian that passes down behind the northern horizon. (And this without prejudice, incidentally, to Professor A. N. dos Santos's much more recent calculation, reported in *Amateur Astronomer and Earth Sciences* of October 1996, that it would also have pointed directly at the star Vega at the beginning of the summer solstice of 11,917 BC.)

Meanwhile Robert Menzies had suggested, as we have seen, not merely that the passageways somehow represented a blueprint for humanity's destiny: it was scaled, he proposed, to a precise 1 Pyramid Inch (1 P") per year.

This would be logical, given that this measurement and its multiple, the Sacred Cubit, are also basic to the exterior design (*see Chapter 4*). But was it true? And if so, was there indeed some kind of internal datum point to measure from?

Piazzi Smyth was well qualified to judge. Having for 20 years now been Astronomer Royal for Scotland, he had all the astronomical tables at his disposal, and considerable practical and computational skills to match. Accordingly, he set out for Giza, armed to the teeth with gadgets, equipment and general paraphernalia. These included a clinkstone measuring standard accurate to a hundredth of an inch, a set of specially-made measuring rods, a measuring bar with built-in thermometers to correct for expansion and contraction due to temperature variations, and a custom-built clinometer for measuring the slopes of the passageways with unprecedented accuracy. Moreover, for photographing the interior he developed entirely new techniques of stereoscopy and magnesium flare photography.

The man was nothing if not thorough.

So, in the event, was his ensuing survey of the Pyramid – much more so, in fact, than any hitherto. And in the course of it he was delighted to discover what Menzies' theory demanded.

The all-important time datum.

The original entrance to the pyramid has long since disappeared. Thanks to centuries of despoliation of the building's polished limestone casing by the local population, it has been first denuded, then mined into deeply. It is as a result of this that a huge limestone gable, originally buried deep within the masonry, is now exposed to view (*see illustration*). It serves no obvious architectural function – which at once suggests some alternative, *symbolic* function. In front of it several further gables once existed, *each succeeding one leaning back further and further into the pyramid* – apparently to the point where, instead of being vertical, they were now perpendicular to the entrance passage (*compare general diagram on page 69*).

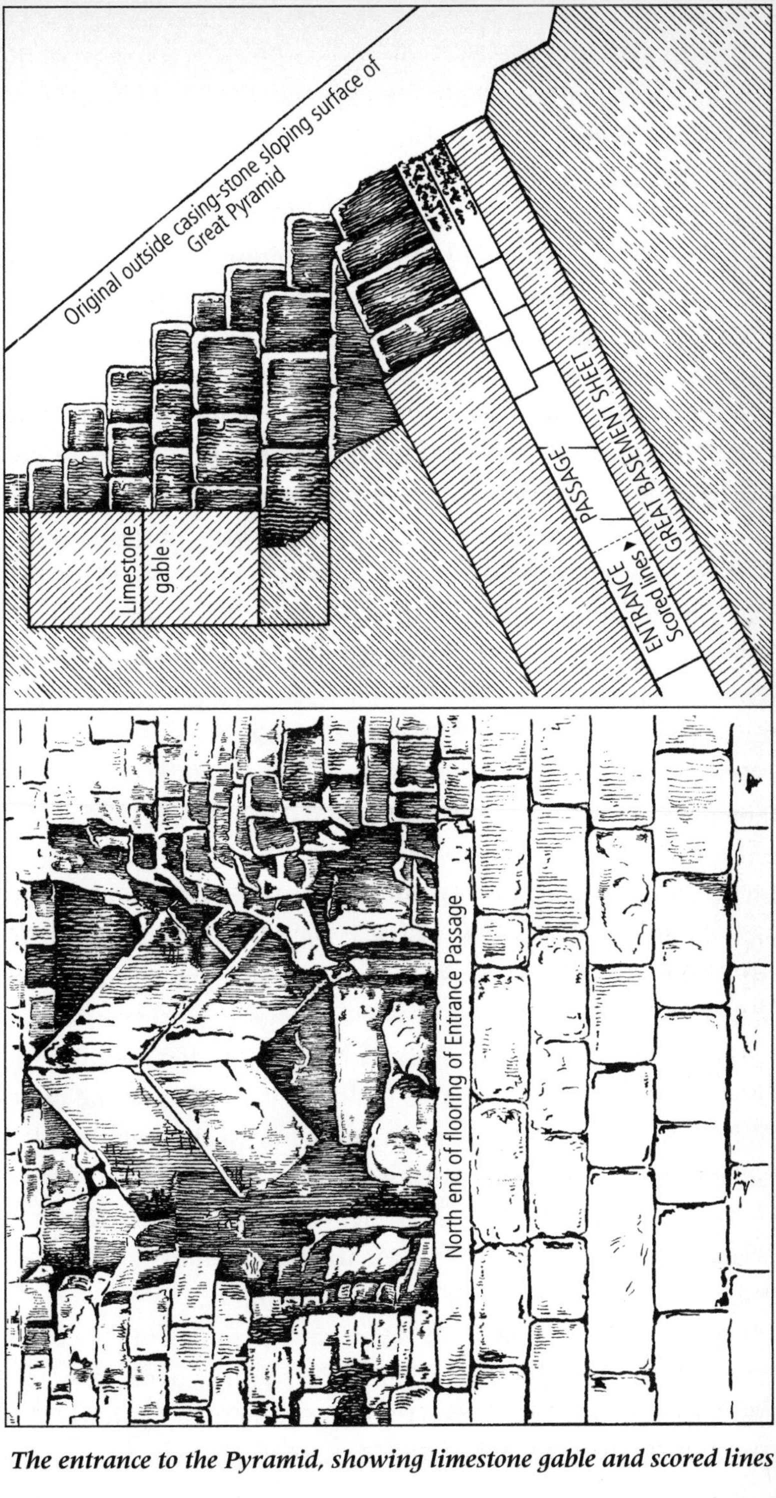
Original outside casing-stone sloping surface of Great Pyramid
Limestone gable
ENTRANCE PASSAGE
Scored lines
GREAT BASEMENT SHEET
North end of flooring of Entrance Passage

The entrance to the Pyramid, showing limestone gable and scored lines

In retrospect, then, the message of their huge, upward-pointing arrowheads is a fairly obvious one. *Refer at this point perpendicularly to the sky overhead*, it seems to say.

And massively and emphatically, too.

The point seems not to have occurred to Smyth. Nevertheless, where his interpretational intuition evidently let him down, his eyes and his sheer thoroughness more than made up for it.

A short distance down the entrance passage from the designed entrance, *and immediately below the culminating gable*, he suddenly noticed two pairs of wall joints which, unlike the sloping joints around them, were almost vertical. The anomaly seemed designed to attract the careful observer's attention. And sure enough, immediately down the slope beyond them a pair of dead straight lines, one on either side of the passage, had been scored opposite each other from roof to floor, *perpendicular to the sloping passage*.

They lay just 481.7457 Pyramid Inches down in from the designed entrance – and it looked remarkably as if they were intended to *calibrate* the passage. But in what way?

Smyth deduced that their function was to define a *plane* – the same plane, in the event, that the original gables had also evidently been doing their best to indicate. Had he but known it at the time, that deduction was fully justified – for at the corresponding point in the Trial Passages (*see diagram page 55*) just such a flat plane offered itself. And its function – whether practical or merely symbolic – seems to have been *to act as a pelorus to sight the stars*.

And so which stars did this plane intersect during the third millennium BC? There could be no doubt about it. During the period in question the only feature of any note to pass through this plane while transiting the meridian (and while Alpha Draconis was at its lower culmination) was Alcyone, chief star of the scintillating Pleiades, or Seven Sisters, which marked the hump of Taurus, the Bull. And it did so at noon of the spring equinox.

It was appropriate. For Taurus was the ruling sign of the current age – the sign in which the vernal sun currently stood.

But *which* spring equinox? Here the computations were complex. Smyth's initial conclusion was that it was the spring equinox of 'very close to 2170 BC'. However, being fully aware of the limitations of the astronomy of his day, and not being of a particularly arrogant turn of mind, he put the problem out for other astronomers to check. Various alternative dates were proposed. But by 1879 it seemed that the true date was 'more nearly 2140 BC'.

On which Smyth, open-minded to the last, commented, 'Very probably.'[31]

Since then, astronomy has made further strides. The possibilities have been further narrowed down. And the upshot is that the astronomical fix for the all-important datum-point is *noon of the spring equinox (21 March) 2141 BC.*[35]

At that moment the Pole Star was passing unseen through the northern meridian. At that moment, too, the Pleiades, equally unseen, were hovering above the entrance passage on the *southern* meridian at an altitude of some 65°. Moreover, some 5° immediately below them, the noonday sun itself was glaring steeply down on the Great Pyramid, making it – as it would continue to do every noon until the following autumn – a building without a shadow.

And from that moment – for the Great Pyramid's internal chronograph, at least – time began.

Now the process of detailed measurement could commence. Retracing the 481.7457 P″ back to the designed entrance on Menzies' proposed inch/year scale gave its symbolic 'dating' as 2623 BC – which (remarkably enough) fell well within the supposed dates of the Pharaoh Khufu, with whom the Pyramid is generally associated. Moreover it marked, of all dates in the year, the summer solstice – which seemed unlikely to have been an accident.

The fact was distinctly encouraging. And it posed the inevitable, intriguing question. What would happen if you now measured *forwards* in time?

The question was answered, equally inevitably, by succeeding generations of pyramidologists. And the upshot was positively overwhelming. The bottom end of the descending passage, as defined by the intersecting plane of the ensuing horizontal passage, marked out the period between AD 1440 and 1521 – the seminal years of the European Renaissance, whose values (and especially its materialist ones) were subsequently to transform the whole world, and not always for the better.

Assuming that the scale of the horizontal passage was now meant to be projected on to the slope (as the corresponding feature in the Trial Passages suggested), the rough-hewn subterranean antechamber, with its carefully sculpted 'roof-fall', next marked out the period from 1767 to 1848 – a revolutionary period during which, for the established world order, the roof did indeed start to cave in.

And the lowly subterranean passage finally debouched into the ghastly subterranean chamber *in the summer of 1914.*

The omens, then, were disturbing. The chamber itself, it was clear, could not help but represent the events of the 20th century and beyond. There was, it seemed, to be a time of severe turbulence, a deep pit, and then (as the dead-end passage revealed) a long period during which humanity could do no more than crawl with difficulty towards final extinction.

Yet there was hope. At a point 688.0245 P″ down the descending passage from the scored lines, the ascending passage began. The dating for its entrance worked out at 30 March 1453 BC. It was, admittedly, blocked by a granite plug. Symbolically, however, it was possible to burrow around this through the softer limestone masonry. To biblical enthusiasts of the time, this was a gift. The granite plug corresponded to the heavy burden imposed by the tablets of the Mosaic Law (which were presumably also of Sinaitic granite), while the passage's top end, 1485.0068 P″ later, clearly marked out 1st April AD 33, *which was evidently the date of the Crucifixion.*

The nexus of the passageways, then, had been reached – a nexus which, as it now transpires, marks not only the period of the BC/AD divide, but also the approximate mid-point of the era between the first date on the Pyramid's chronograph and the astronomical Last Time of Osiris (*see Chapter 3*).

Now the roof height suddenly soared in seven stages to a lofty 286.1 P″ above the ascending passage's roof-line – the same 286.1 P″ (or 7.2747 metres) by which the Pyramid had been 'built small'

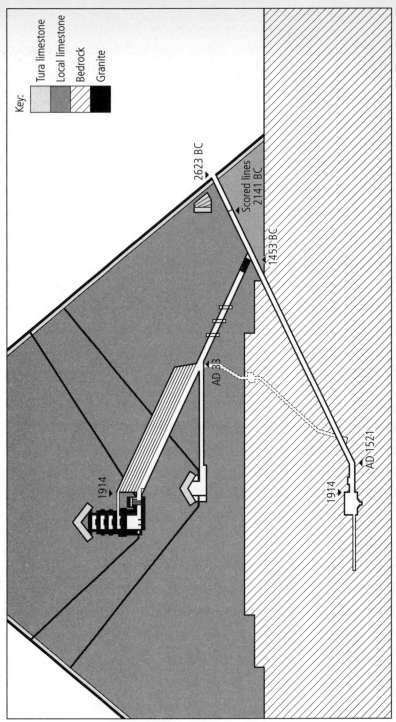

Key:
- Tura limestone
- Local limestone
- Bedrock
- Granite

2623 BC

Scored lines
2141 BC

1453 BC

AD 33

AD 1521

1914

1914

Overview of the Great Pyramid's apparent chronograph

as determined by Piazzi Smyth and his early successors

and the whole passage system had been offset to the east, or left of centre – until, 1881.2223 P″ later, the floorline of the magnificent and, frankly, dizzying Grand Gallery terminated at its south wall, indicating the summer of 1914 – *once again, squarely on the summer solstice (22 June)*.

Thus far, it has to be admitted, the upshot was stunning. Yet, from this point on, various worrying imponderables made further decoding difficult. Merely continuing to measure on the same scale would have placed the south wall of the King's Chamber – the evident terminus of the whole project – just 475.40072 years after the summer solstice of 1914, at the beginning of the year 2390. Yet on this basis humanity would as early as 1972 have started to undergo the strange events apparently indicated by the antechamber – which, as we shall see, subsequent experience seems not to have confirmed. Besides, the floor from this point on was horizontal, not (as previously) on the slope: much of it, too, was made of granite, not limestone – and either fact could be significant for the existing timescale. More to the point, a step (either the so-called Great Step itself or the geometrical 'hidden step' beneath it) had now intervened – and there was more than a suspicion that a step might indicate an actual *change of timescale*.

Seizing on the idea, indeed, several early 20th-century enthusiasts went on to propose that the scale changed at this point to one *month* per year. And true enough, on this basis the first section of low passageway leading to the King's Chamber corresponded to the period from 1914–18 – the exact period, as grisly events would go on to reveal, of the First World War. Unfortunately, however, on the same scale the culmination of the passage system – the apparent 'end of the world for upper-path humanity' – would come in August 1953.

Clearly, unless it has come and gone unnoticed, nothing of the kind has happened.

Much the same problem affected the exact timing of the evidently even grislier events portrayed in the subterranean chamber, while the Queen's Chamber and its passage, on the same basis, remained a complete mystery.

It was 1977, in fact, before I was able to suggest a consistent and apparently watertight formula for interpreting these various anomalies.[19] In the case of the various steps, this involved a scale change based (logically enough) on the height of the step and the base unit of the previous scale. In the case of granite floors, the scale was evidently based not on the Pyramid Inch, but on the standard one-hundredth subdivision of the Royal Cubit known as the n – which meant that the King's Chamber, with its north-south width of 10 Royal Cubits, appropriately represented an age of a thousand years.

And so it was that the Great Pyramid's chronograph was gradually revealed for what it evidently was. The 'air shafts' had primed the gun. The polar entrance passage had aimed it. The scored lines had pulled the trigger.

And the rest was quite literally history.

However the ancient lords of Giza had managed to do it, then, the Pyramid was indeed coded for time.

But might it be coded for much else as well?

10

THE
SECRET
KEY

CLEARLY, IT MAKES NO MORE SENSE TO SAY *WHEN* WITHOUT SAYING *WHAT* than it does to day *what* without saying *when*. The one without the other is meaningless. Space cannot exist without time, nor time without space. History, as even teachers have recently started to realize, is more than just a succession of dates.

Any designer of the Great Pyramid who was clever enough to encode time into his building, in other words, must surely have been clever enough to encode what was timed as well. The Pyramid must reflect actual developments on the ground.

True, this does pose major questions. How could whoever it was possibly have *known* all this? Was the designer a prophet? Did he or she expect the design somehow to *control* events? Or was it something that had already occurred before, possibly in an unending cycle? Of the three possibilities, the last may well turn out to be nearest the mark – though, as we shall see, in a perhaps rather surprising way.

However, theorizing as to the *how* should not prevent us from looking at the *what*, any more than it prevented us looking at the *when* in the previous chapter. We humans lived in the world, after all, for long ages before we ever got around to explaining it.

And so what signs are there of some kind of secret code?

Clearly, if there is one, it can operate only in terms of shapes and sizes, of slopes and directions, of stone types and textures, of measurements and multiples, of figures and fractions. There is simply nothing else to decipher. Once again the designer seems to have foreseen that no script or written document was likely to survive the depredations of the ages. Only the brute facts of the design were likely to last, ready to be decoded once human civilization reached a stage of learning and insight adequate to the task.

The chances were, after all, that only when that level had been reached would humanity be up to the task of responding to it with the panoply of advanced technologies that, as we shall go on to see, would be essential for doing so.

In fact we have already encountered several likely elements of such a code. We know that the full-design Pyramid itself signifies Planet Earth in its ideal state. We have concluded that the passageways signify humanity's experience of Earth. We deduced from the Pyramid's astronomical co-ordinates that that experience is timed to link in with events during the third millennium BC. We were forced by the scored lines, in fact, to conclude that it meshes in with history precisely at the vernal equinox of 2141 BC. We have further deduced that movement southwards through the passageways signifies movement through time. We have little option but to accept – provisionally, at least – Menzies' theory that one Pyramid Inch corresponds to a year, at least on sloping, limestone floors.

But that is not all.

The Great Pyramid, as we noted earlier, was deliberately 'built small'. The perimeter as constructed fell short of the ideal perimeter (indicated by the foundation sockets and the concavity of the surviving core masonry) by 286.1 Pyramid Inches (P″). The base perimeter of the missing full-design capstone would seemingly have measured 2288.817 P″, or 8 × 286.1 P″. The passageways lie 286.1 P″ to the east, of left, of the building's centreline. The Grand

Gallery's roofline is 286.1 P″ above that of the ascending passage that leads into it.

Clearly, then, this particular distance is meant to be significant – significant enough to lead us from the outside of the building into its interior. And since, in a minus or leftward direction, it seems to signify *lack of completeness*, its application in a positive or rightward direction would seem to represent the regaining of that completeness.

Which immediately begs to identify the code significance of left and right as well.

Meanwhile each base side of the Pyramid necessarily falls short of the ideal length by just a quarter of that distance – which means that at each end it misses the designed corner by an eighth of it, or 35.76 P″. This distance, too, is represented inside the passage system – notably in the original height of the Great Step at the top end of the Grand Gallery, which is of course encountered *further on* than the vertical distance of 286.1 P″ at its lower end.

The distance 35.76 P″ seems to have some connection, then, with the idea of *result*, as would the quantity 8. Thus, both deserve to be included in any reconstructed code.

Meanwhile the full-design Pyramid is of course five-sided (including the base) and five-pointed – which might indicate that the number 5, too, stands in some way for completeness or perfection. So that 40, or 8 times 5, might then indicate in some way the *result of perfection*.

This process of continuing deduction is inevitably a slow and distinctly meditative business. One thing, as the saying has it, leads to another. Squareness or rectangularity leads to fourness. Circularity leads to π, or even to the number 3. 3 leads to 9, or 3^2. Limestone leads to granite, and granite interrupts limestone, as though the one stands for Earth and the other for heaven (in whatever guise).

But eventually everything seems to slot into place. Almost everything turns out to have a meaning. And the resulting reconstructed code can be set out in tabular form:

THE GREAT PYRAMID:
TENTATIVE CODE-RECONSTRUCTION

P″ = Pyramid Inch (2.5427 cm): SC = Sacred Cubit (25 P″): RC = Royal Cubit (20.6066 P″)

General

Great Pyramid	Planet Earth
Capstone (missing)	completion, perfection, illumination
Passageways	life-paths through Earth from 3rd millennium BC
North-south axis	balance, cosmic harmony
One-third height	balance, cosmic harmony

Directional

Southward	progress through time
Off-centre	loss of balance and harmony
Down/left/east	falling away from balance and harmony
Up/right/west	return to balance and harmony

Features

Sloping passages		human evolution through time
Horizontal passages		events at given levels of evolutionary consciousness
Steps		changes of timescale
	up	more years per P″
	down	less years per P″
	vertical	new scale based on height and previous scale
	non-vertical	new scale based on projection of old, sloping scale on to horizontal
	mid-passage	movable
Limestone		physical, material, terrestrial
Granite		supraphysical, hyperconscious, non-terrestrial, advanced intelligence
Chambers		culminating ages
	gabled	ages or dimensions of wholeness and integration
	non-gabled	preparatory ages or dimensions short of final perfection
'Air shafts'	northern	channels of ingress
	southern	channels of emergence

'Telescopic' structures	explosive inner development
Portcullises	interventions from 'above'
Gables	upward-pointing arrowheads
Scored lines	datum for chronograph

Levels

Subterranean chamber roof	plane of despair and darkness
Queen's chamber floor	plane of dawning re-integration
Queen's chamber 'airshaft' outlets (Pyramid's $^1/_2$-height)	plane of semi-emergence
Summit platform (sum of King's Chamber outlet courses)	plane of potential escape and cosmic reintegration

Geometric

1 P″	one year in sloping passages
20.6066 P″ (1 RC)	mortality, physicality
25 P″ (1 SC)	total perfection ($= 5^2$)
29.84P″	death
33.5 P″	transformation, transformer
35.763 P″	effect of earlier change of consciousness
37.995 P″	death
41.21 P″ (2 RC)	mortality
286.1 P″	loss or regaining of balance and integration
365.242 P″	time
1881.2 P″	quantum leap of consciousness
5448.736 P″	incompleteness, but pregnant with possible perfection and fulfilment
26° 18′ 9.7″ (polar angle)	evolutionary progress or decline
51° 51′ 14.3″ (casing angle)	ultimate wholeness and perfection
Square/rectangle	physical, material, terrestrial
Circle	supraphysical, non-terrestrial
Circle superimposed on square of equal area	total integration of higher and lower consciousness

Arithmetical

1	unity, oneness
2	productive
3	perfect, utter, whole, super-dimensional
π	infinity, superdimensionality, space
4	physical, material, Earth
5	completion, perfection, illumination
6	incompleteness, preparation
7 (4 + 3)	fusion of upper and lower consciousness
8	manifestation, result
9 (3^2)	utter perfection or completeness: total superdimensionality
10	age, era
11	realization, achievement
12	humanity
13	higher self, superdimensional consciousness
19	death, mortality
25 (5^2)	total perfection/ illumination
153	enlightenment, transformation
+/-	plus/minus, add/subtract
×/÷	of/by or through
Squared	total, utter
Square root	essence or seed of

Various criticisms could of course be levelled at the code as listed. One might be the extraordinary and (some may say) unrealistic degree of precision claimed, both for the code itself and for the building's measurements as referred to previously. Yet the fact is that the Great Pyramid has been far more thoroughly surveyed than any other building on Earth – clear evidence in itself, if evidence were needed, that people have long suspected the monument of being much more than it seems. The figures produced by the surveyors and astronomers have in turn been checked by the engineers, who have corrected the raw data for observed subsidence, distortion, erosion, wear and exfoliation. Their figures in turn have been corrected (for the presumed original design) by the mathematicians, bearing in mind the building's obvious π-proportions and evident

Earth-commensurate geometry. The sheer exigencies of trigonom-
etry have then produced very precise figures indeed for the measurements of the whole passage system, which in side-elevation
traces a clear and precise geometrical figure within the building's
general outline.

True, these figures are theoretical. But – especially as listed by
Rutherford[35] – they are sound. In fact, they are for all intents and
purposes definitive. And the fact that the irrational quantity π is
fundamental to the whole design means, of course, that each measurement can be calculated to a theoretically infinite degree of ex-
actitude.

Thus, 20.6066 P″ really does mean 20.6066 P″, and 26° 18′ 9.7″
really does mean 26° 18′ 9.7″ – even though this latter is a less
steep angle for the descending passage than that currently obtaining, thanks to a foot or so of subsidence under the building's centre
and two large earthquakes during the Middle Ages.

Nevertheless, there are clear signs that, in the case of linear
measurements, what really counts is the number of *complete Pyramid Inches*. The figures, as a result, may be found to have been
rounded down (contrary to the more familiar modern mathematical
practice of rounding up). Thus, there are a number of cases where
the code-distance 29.84 P″, for example, seems to be represented
by a measurement of only 29 P″.

All distances listed under the geometric code, in other words,
may be regarded as having 'rounded down' equivalents in the
arithmetical code.

But mathematical over-exactness is not the only cause for possible criticism. Many people may feel that the code as it stands is
'too religious by half' – and certainly too religious to be likely. Actually, it is not half as religious as my original reconstruction of it
in my book *The Great Pyramid Decoded*.[19] The Pyramidologists, after
all, were convinced that the Pyramid was nothing less than the
Bible in stone (notwithstanding the fact that, chronologically, it
would have had to be the other way around, with the Bible being
the Pyramid on paper). Inevitably, therefore, the established vo-
cabulary for discussing the message of the passageways and their

presumed message was religious. My initial efforts were merely intended to show that, if it *was* religious, then the Pyramid was saying much more than conventional Christians were prepared to allow.

However, even in the world outside the Great Pyramid, there are dangers in using religious language. The first is that the non-religious will not understand it. The second is that the religious, for their part, will assume that they do. To the latter, in fact – and especially to Christians of a Protestant persuasion – the map of spirituality has long since become linguistically fixed, to the point where it risks becoming merely a branch of conventional materialism.

It is not their fault. It is just that, thanks to the return to written sources that characterized the European Renaissance, their tradition has long denied expressly that Truth can be found anywhere but in the Bible. The whole of heaven and hell, of human consciousness and spirituality, is to be found within the pages of a book. Eternity and infinity have been reduced to mere black marks on a page.

It has to be said that, if such attitudes had persisted in science, then modern scientists, like their early Renaissance colleagues, would still be seeking the causes of disease in Galen, or the origins of the universe in Aristotle.

Thus, religious language is dangerous. In my second book on the subject, therefore,[20] I sought to avoid it. Instead, I resorted primarily to the language of psychology. But of course psychology is a religion in its own right. It has its own characteristic beliefs and rituals, its own temples and high priests. Freud and Jung are as widely revered in their sphere as Moses and Jesus in theirs. Even their hieratic roles are viewed by disciples in a similar light. And so once again I courted the charge of over-religiosity.

The above table represents a further attempt, and hopefully a final one. Yet even here, it may be claimed, religiosity has left its traces. It is a bland, 'New Age' type of religiosity, admittedly – but religiosity for all that.

If that is indeed the impression, then I have to plead diminished responsibility. For the amount of religiosity in the code list seems to me to represent an irreducible minimum. *The Great Pyramid's message, in other words, is inescapably 'religious'.*

This does not of course mean that it is merely a branch of conventional religion. Still less does it justify the Pyramidologists' traditional claims. It does mean, however (as we shall see later), that the message is deeply serious and highly idealistic in tone, and touches on the very destiny of the human soul.

The fact that religion has long since co-opted all such matters and claimed them for its own does not of itself mean that the Pyramid's message is merely religious, however. Still less is there any question of 'reading religion into the Pyramid's message'. Quite the reverse, in fact. We have already noted the existence of distinct hints that things may very well be the other way around. Many of the concepts that are basic to religion, in other words, may well have derived in the first place, via a variety of ancient mythologies, from the Great Pyramid itself and the original designers of the great Giza project. It is the religious concepts that may be half-remembered distortions of the ancient message, rather than the reverse.

This might help to explain why so much that was basic to Egypt's ancient Osirian religion crops up again in Greek mythology, in early Mithraism and in the salvationist aspects of Christianity, no less than it does in the native traditions of Tibet and Central America.[13] Perhaps it is not entirely insignificant, indeed, that both Moses and Jesus are reported to have spent time *in Egypt*.

But then neither the code nor the Pyramid's evident message is specific as to level of interpretation. Much as with the Bible itself, much depends on the assumptions that you bring to it in the first place. Orthodox Jews, who naturally have their own set of assumptions about what are, after all, their own scriptures, are constantly amazed at the constructions that Christians manage to place upon them – much as an Englishman might be surprised to be told by a Frenchman what cricket is about merely on the basis of the latest edition of Wisden. Yet a modern seeker who has forsaken Christianity to undertake a pilgrimage through Hinduism and Buddhism will return to the Bible to discover yet another set of insights – and one that will certainly be news to both Jews *and* Christians.

The same goes for the prophecies of Nostradamus. What you see depends to a large extent on how you look at them. The old tradition that we see the world by the light of our own eyes, in short, has a lot to be said for it.

In all such cases, however, by far the best plan is clearly to approach the problem with a completely open mind. It may not be easy. In the absence of our familiar prejudices we are apt to feel naked. Perhaps that is why Jesus advised that we approach our destiny with the attitude of a little child.

Yet it has to be attempted – and this means sticking to the facts on the ground.

There is, it seems, a chronograph. There seems to be a secret code, or key. The key once in place, then, there is only one thing left to be done.

And that is to turn it.

11

A PROSPECT
OF DOOM

THE PLACE TO INSERT THE KEY, naturally, is in the door. And certainly it is at the entrance to the Great Pyramid that we need to begin our code read-out. Some of it will necessarily be fairly technical, but the reader is, of course, at liberty to skip to the summaries in bold type as the mood dictates.

We have already noted some of the more prominent features (which are listed in full in my original book on the subject, *The Great Pyramid Decoded*[19]). The centreline of the entrance lies not on the earth-symbolizing Pyramid's north-south axis, but 286.1 P" to the left, or east of it. Moreover, it coincides with the designed Pyramid's 19th course of masonry. But there is more. It is just 37.995 P" high and 41.21 P" wide.

On referring to the code, then, its significance becomes perfectly clear.

Here begins the path of those mortals who are destined for death by virtue of having lost their natural balance and harmony with the universe.

There is even a possible hint that that imbalance may lie in an over-emphasis of left-brain – i.e. exclusively language-based – thinking.

101

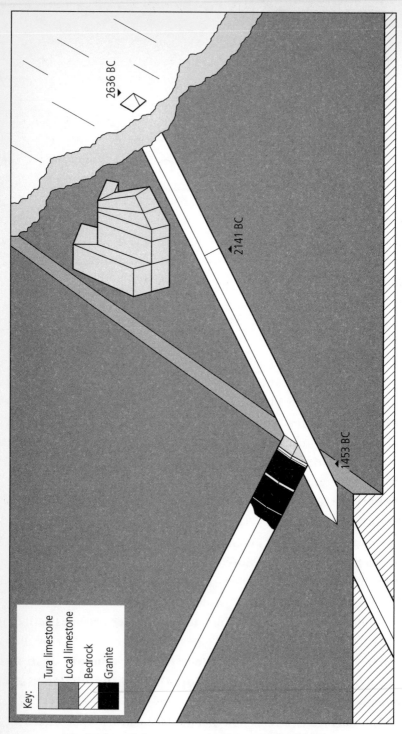

2636 BC

2141 BC

1453 BC

Key:

Tura limestone

Local limestone

Bedrock

Granite

Projection of the entrance and descending passage

The long descending passage now follows. 41.21 P″ wide, it is constructed in limestone and rectangular in cross section. The angle of slope is 26° 18′ 9.7″ from the horizontal. Calibrated (as we have seen) to the vernal equinox of 2141 BC, it actually starts at a point denoting the summer solstice of 2623 BC. Once again, therefore, a clear read-out is possible.

A long evolutionary decline for terrestrial mortals will be in progress as early as 2623 BC.

At a point 481.7457 P″ down the floorline of the passageway, two straight lines are scored perpendicularly to the slope in either wall, preceded by two anomalous, near-vertical joints. These lines mark the plane of Alpha Draconis at the spring equinox (21 March) of 2141 BC. We have already established their likely significance.

This is the 'go' mark. Start measuring and counting from here.

688.0245 P″ further on still, the passage floor reaches a point directly under the sill of an *ascending* passage which now bores up into the Pyramid's masonry from the passage roof. Originally concealed by a prismatic slab of limestone, this entrance is only some 38 P″ (2 x 19) wide.

Any attempt to reverse the general decline is likely to encounter physical difficulties which may threaten death. Nevertheless, the attempt will be made on or about 30 March 1453 BC.

The passage now continues its long descent into the limestone bedrock beneath the Pyramid for a further 2675.006 P″. At this point it intersects the level of the subterranean chamber roof (*see below*). But just above this level a rough opening in the right-hand wall allows access to an irregular shaft that leads up, first through the bedrock and then through the Pyramid's masonry, to the central junction of the upper passageways (*see next chapter*).

By AD 1223 such a level of human degeneration will have been reached as almost to be beyond redemption. Even only marginally above this level, however, a path of recovery will remain available.

At a point 286.1 P″ further down the slope, the passage floor finally reaches symbolic 'rock bottom' as it intersects the subterranean passage floorline.

Given that all balance and integration has been lost, the stage is set for a lasting dispensation of darkness and despair, commencing in the year 1521.

This latter date seems to mark the European Renaissance and Reformation, both of which were later to have such huge effects on attitudes – and especially materialistic attitudes – all over the world.

The new, horizontal subterranean chamber passage leads southwards through a rough-hewn antechamber with carefully sculpted 'roof fall' (dated for 1767 to 1848) to the great subterranean chamber, into which it tumbles 352.2933 P″ after its intersection with the descending passage floorline. Tunnelled entirely through the natural limestone, the passage is rectangular in cross section, only 35.76 P″ high (insufficient for standing) and, at 33.5 P″ wide, appreciably narrower than the descending passage.

Having reached rock bottom, terrestrial humanity will now stumble along at a low level, transformed into an inferior life form as a result of its initial loss of balance and harmony. After 'the roof falls in' between 1767 and 1848, an era of 'hell on earth' will be entered in the summer of 1914.

The celebrated era of revolutions encompassing not only the American and French revolutions, but the Napoleonic wars, the subsequent French revolution of 1830 and the *six* European revolutions of 1848 is thus well marked out, as apparently is the onset of the First World War.

Entered by a large downward drop or 'step' – while the roof height rises by 89.80568 P″ (code equivalent of 3 × 29.84 P″) – the great subterranean chamber is by far the largest chamber in the Pyramid, stretching westwards well beyond the Pyramid's north-south centreline. Carved out of the solid limestone, its floor is low at the eastern end – where it is interrupted by a symbolic ravine leading to a deep pit – and high in its western part, where it is marked by a series of high ridges separated by gulleys running east

Pyramidologist John Edgar sets the scale at the junction between the descending and subterranean passages

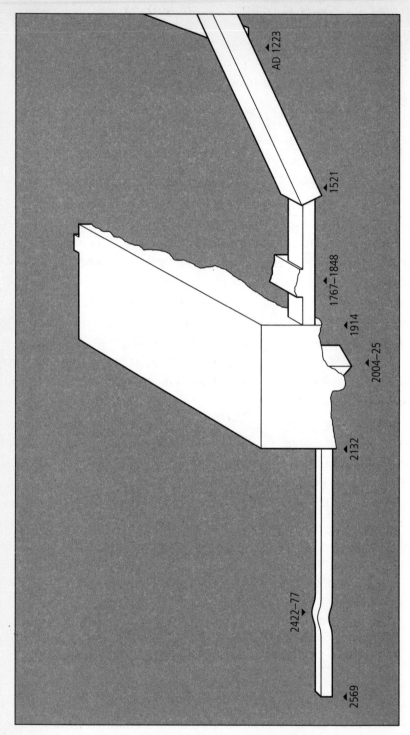

Projection of the subterranean complex

to west. Its flat roof lies 1881.2 P″ below the plane of the Queen's Chamber floor. It measures 322.7711 P″ across, at which point the dead-end passage exits further southward, its floor level, 41.21 P″ below the level of the subterranean passage floor, apparently suggesting that the initial drop at the entrance to the chamber is to be regarded as a downward step of 2 Royal Cubits. The upper part of the pit is 67.59 P″ deep (equivalent to 2×33.5 P″) and its lower part 41.2 P″ deep, making a total depth of 108.8 P″ (code-equivalent of 9×12). In the west wall a blind recess seems to symbolize the continuing availability of the 'well shaft'.

Terrestrial humanity will now enter an era of 'hell on earth' and utter death, marked by a level of consciousness that is a quantum leap of consciousness below that necessary for the dawning of re-integration. During it, the risk of falling headlong into a bottomless pit of consequential death can be avoided only by turning to the right and working towards some kind of balance, thus obtaining entry into one of the alternative, higher paths. This era will terminate in December, 2132.

Clearly, then, this era is our own. There are evidently severe crises and catastrophes to come. Crude mapping of the chamber appears to date the 'bottomless pit' to 2004, and its deepest part to 2010. Its southern wall is reached in 2025, a halfway step out of it attained by 2075, and levels of achievement not far short of those in the earlier part of the chamber reached by 2100. Evidently, then, if the portrayal is correct, we should expect the bottom to fall out of our familiar, materialist world for at least 20 years during the early part of the 21st century, though the datings are likely to be accurate only to some ±3 years.

The final, dead-end passage now bores yet further southwards through the limestone bedrock on a line 1.2114 P″ to the east of the axis of the rest of the passage system. Its floor lies 41.21 P″ below that of the original subterranean chamber passage. Only 29.8412 P″ square in cross section, it offers crawling room for some 420 P″ before taking a slight 'kink' to the west for some 84 P″. It then continues to a dead-end in the rock, 645.5422 P″ from

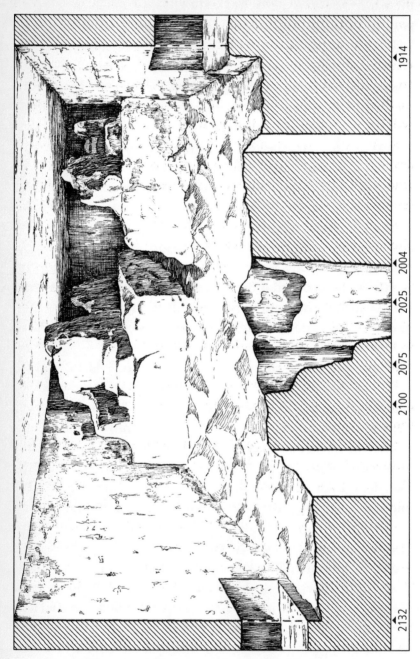

The great subterranean chamber, looking west

with foreground cut out to expose pit

its own entrance and 5448.736 P″ from the original entrance to the whole passage system. *This is exactly the same distance, as it happens, as that between the Pyramid's base and its summit platform.*

Terrestrial humanity will now enter a lowly, animal path which – despite some movement towards regeneration between 2422 and 2477 – will lead to final physical extinction in the autumn of 2569. At this point terrestrial evolution will have gone as far as it can go.

Such, then, (failing any effort at self-improvement and self-development) is the path evidently mapped out for humanity by whoever left us the Pyramid's stupendous message in stone. It represents the lowest path of all.

And the message is clear. Should we fail collectively to use our phenomenal mental, spiritual and physical powers positively, they will instead spell doom for us. Especially should we beware, it seems, of misusing those mental powers that are focused by such left-brain activities as language and rational thought. Like nuclear technology, they offer us almost unlimited powers for either good or evil – and should we choose to ignore the one, the other will inevitably take over.

Perhaps, indeed, our nuclear technology offers the ultimate example of this, so that it would not be too surprising if it also in some way proved our chosen instrument of doom.

It is a sobering message, and an even more sobering destiny. But fortunately, as we shall see, they are not the only ones on offer. The ancient gods of Giza, if gods they were, seemingly had yet other possibilities in mind.

How would it be, then, if – just for a moment – we lifted our eyes from the monuments of Egypt to contemplate those mysterious Lords of Orion themselves?

STARWATCH
ONE

WHAT LORDLY CIVILIZATION *could possibly be at work here? What
high intelligence could have such concern for human posterity? Who is it
who presumes to call down such a catalogue of doom upon us?*

It is legitimate to speculate.

*Clearly, their technology is of a high order. Their ability to manipulate
huge weights is awesome. Their surveying techniques are immaculate.
Their knowledge of the solar system is breathtaking. Their knowledge of
the stars is stunning. But why should they wish to link the stars so closely
to earth in the way displayed at Giza?*

*True, the precessional cycle makes it possible to use the stars as time
markers that will be valid for thousands of years. That much is obvious.
But why choose the constellation Orion rather than any other pattern of
stars as your signature on the ground? The answer 'Because Orion was
Osiris' will not do – for Orion assuredly came first, Osiris afterwards.*

*Any other pattern, after all, would have done just as well. But Orion
has a special attraction. The three almost equidistant bright stars of the
Hunter's belt – from left to right, Al Nitak, Al Nilam and Mintaka – mark
out a very nearly straight line in the night sky. Yet straight lines as regular
as this are rarely seen in nature. That is what makes Orion perhaps the*

most easily recognized of all the constellations. But this immediately poses an intriguing question.

Just how natural is this particular straight line?

A civilization that can evidently move mountains might just possibly be advanced enough to move whole worlds as well. Some kind of gravity-control technology could explain both. In which case, a vast demonstration of cyclopeanism such as that at Giza would be an excellent way of telling others that it has that technology.

But if worlds, what of larger bodies, too? Could some advanced intelligence be pushing the very stars around? And if so, could it be the selfsame intelligence that we are encountering here?

One of the most obvious ways for an advanced, galactic civilization to signal its presence, after all, would indeed be to engineer the stars. Place three major stars in a stable straight line, and that presence would be proclaimed throughout the galaxy. And true it is that Al Nitak and Al Nilam (the two left-hand stars) are part of a family cluster, steadily travelling together through space (as Sir James Jeans put it)[16] 'like a flight of swans through a confused crowd of rooks and starlings'. Mintaka, too, is evidently a fellow traveller – though it is twice as far away from us.

Are they still working on the problem? Or has Mintaka been knocked out of line by other gravitational attractions during its long passage through the galaxy?

Or – an even more stupendous possibility – is the difference deliberate?

A simple straight line, after all, would advertise your presence throughout the galaxy. But displace just one of your three stars, and you in effect beam your advertisement to **one particular** area of the galaxy only. In the case of the stars of Orion's belt, that particular galactic quadrant is ours. Or rather, it includes both us and the area immediately to our galactic south. The corresponding area immediately beyond Orion's belt is, of course, also targeted.

But why us, when there is the whole of the rest of the galaxy to aim at, its hundred billion stars possibly swarming with life-bearing planets? The answer may very well be that we are the nearest of them. For the sun and the stars of Orion all share the same 'local' arm of the galaxy. In galactic terms, we are near neighbours.

It would be no wonder, then, if the message were deliberately beamed in our direction.

But in that case, by whom?

Whether the ancient founding gods were human or non-human we can but guess at present. But that their achievements were of a vastly higher order than our own can scarcely be doubted. Neither can the fact that they were once on Earth and now are not.

Thus, once having left their indelible mark, they may simply have died out. Or possibly only their local agents did – some advanced civilization of the stamp of the semi-legendary Atlantis, perhaps. In the light of their vast intelligence and titanic technology, however, it seems a good deal more likely that they themselves survived. Yet if they survived, they are certainly no longer of this world.

Have those ancient gods, then, long since departed – or perhaps re-departed – for the stars? Are they even now active somewhere out there in the cosmos?

Possibly the Great Pyramid will in due course give us the answer.

What is certain, however, is that we and they have much business together. Their message, whether historically remote or present and actual, is **for us**. *It concerns our future, our prospects, even our very survival.*

It behoves us, then, to take them seriously. Whether in the flesh or merely through their mighty artefacts, they exist for us. We need to relate to them. And so we should do well to find a name for them. We might, for example, call them by the name of the Egyptian **Shemsu-Hor**, *the 'followers of Horus'.*

But there is a more familiar story of our origins – a biblical one that assigns to the creator gods the Hebrew name **Elohim**. *Perhaps, then, 'the Elohim' is what we should call them.*

Until, that is, we finally meet them face to face and learn their **true** *name.*

12

THE
PATHS
OF
<u>HOPE</u>

ALL IS NOT LOST, HOWEVER. From the spring of 2141 BC, as we have seen, new possibilities are set to open up for humanity, initially blocked though they may at first appear to be.

The 38 P"-wide entrance of the ascending passage was original-ly blocked by a prismatic slab of limestone that served to conceal it from anyone passing down the descending passage. Disturbed by the hammering of the Caliph Al-Mamun's excavating workmen some metres to the right on the Pyramid's centreline, the block fell in the ninth century of our era, so revealing to them the true, off-set position of the passageways.

Once again, then, the code suggests a straightforward read-out. **The upward path for terrestrial humanity marked out for the spring of 1453 BC will not at first be apparent.**

Beyond the limestone slab, the tapered ascending passage broadens out to the usual width of 41.21 P" and starts to ascend at the usual angle of 26° 18' 9.7" through the Pyramid's limestone masonry. Immediately, however, it is blocked by a triple granite plug built into the tapered passageway. The upper two blocks are in contact with each other, but there is a gap between the middle

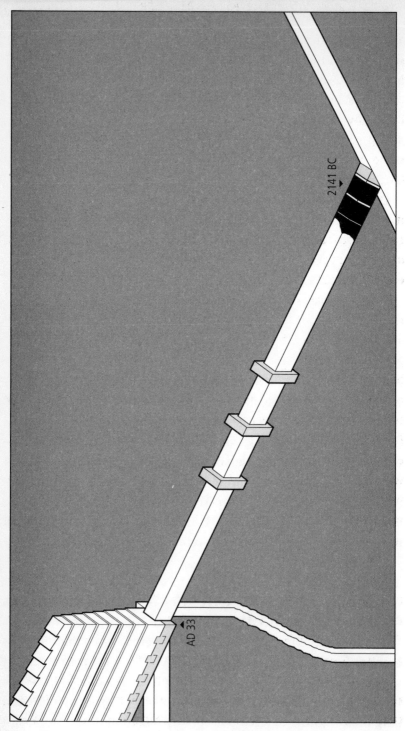

Projection of the ascending passage

and bottom ones. Their lateral dimensions are as for the passage it-self. The total length of the granite plug seems originally to have been 10 RC, but the uppermost block appears to have been much mutilated and consequently shortened. Since the blocks cannot be removed and are theoretically too hard to penetrate, the way ahead has to involve burrowing through the surrounding lime-stone masonry. Originally, further limestone blocks reportedly blocked the remainder of the passage.

Once entered, this new path of evolutionary improve-ment for mortals will be irretrievably blocked by supraphysi-cal or non-terrestrial demands that will prove impossible to accept. Progress will still be possible, however, if physical, earthly efforts are substituted.

Pyramidological commentators without number have linked this new initiative with the celebrated Israelite Exodus from Egypt and the imposition by Moses – and the initial rejection by his peo-ple – of the stern demands of the Torah, or divine Law. The granite blocks, divided into two groups, even recall the twin stone tablets of Sinaitic granite on which that Law is alleged to have been writ-ten. And certainly the proposed dating can be squared with a 'High Date' Exodus. But then other, similar developments were in train elsewhere at the time, too. In India, particularly, the Vedic laws were being written down. The time was right, it seems, for the physical codification of life in the service of religion. The physical must be made to serve the spiritual, even at the risk of substituting mere ritual acts for true awakening.

The passage now continues to ascend through a series of vertical 'girdle stones' that encircle the passageway and anchor it to the building's core masonry, until, 1451.4952 P" after its beginning, the floorline intersects the plane of the Queen's Chamber floor. Then, 33.5 P" further on, the roof line suddenly rises by 286.1 P" at the entrance to the astonishing, corbelled Grand Gallery.

Further physical efforts to drive an upward path through the physical world will ensure that those mortals following this route will reach a level of dawning re-integration in 2 BC. This path will finally attain its culmination on 1st April,

AD 33, when a sudden explosive initiative on the part of a transformer (or a transforming, explosive initiative) will contribute hugely to restoring humanity's balance and reintegration with the cosmos.

Once again biblical enthusiasts are not slow to pinpoint the events apparently referred to. The first of these dates, they claim, represents the birth of Jesus of Nazareth, and the second his crucifixion. And indeed, the dates do seem to fit,[35] as do the symbolic consequences. Yet, once again, other salvationist initiatives were in the air at the time, too, notably within Mahayana Buddhism.

With the entry into the Grand Gallery, all kinds of extraordinary things now start to happen. Initially, the ascending floor simply continues for a further 25 P″, terminating in a small notch or 'peak' that once served to retain a bridging floorslab which sealed off the Queen's Chamber passage (*see next chapter*). To the right, a low tunnel beneath a missing ramp-stone, with its N–S axis 35.76 P″ beyond the Gallery's south wall and its floor on the level of the Queen's Chamber floor, leads the explorer to the right, only to tumble at a point that lies 89.61 P″ further on (code equivalent: 3 x 29.84 P″) – measured from axis to axis – into the top end of the 'well shaft' leading down to the lower passageways (*see previous chapter*). Overhead, the roof height has suddenly leapt upwards by 286.1 P″, while the 1836 P″-long roof (code equivalent: 153 x 12) displays 40 (8 x 5) separate blocks of limestone set ratchet-wise, evidently so as to anchor them into the Pyramid's masonry.

After an initial gap (corresponding to the entrance gangway of the Queen's Chamber passage) the Gallery's central floor simply represents a continuation of that of the ascending passage, whose width of 41.21 P″ (or 2 RC) it exactly mirrors. On either side of it, however, rise two ramps, each 20.61 P″ (or 1 RC) wide – making a total width over the top of them of 4 RC. Above each of these, a series of inset-stones crossed by strange depressions are inserted vertically in each side wall, with corresponding rectangular holes let into the ramps below. Each of these measures 20.61 P″ across, alternately horizontally and on the slope. The bottom hole on the

The Great Sphinx of Giza
Note the rainwater gulleys in back and sides

The Great Pyramid at evening, from the north-west
with the Sphinx just beyond the summit

The Great Pyramid, north-east arris-edge

The constellation of Orion

right: **Giza: the pristine
complex from the north-west
in ancient times**

The young Albert Einstein

Al Nitak and the Horsehead nebula

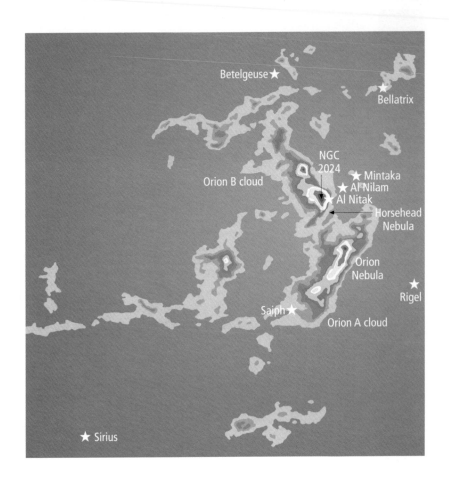

Betelgeuse ★

Bellatrix ★

NGC
2024

★ Mintaka
★ Al Nilam

Orion B cloud

Al Nitak

Horsehead
Nebula

Orion
Nebula

Rigel ★

Saiph ★

Orion A cloud

★ Sirius

Gas-clouds in Orion
Bright colours indicate hotspots

The entry into the Grand Gallery

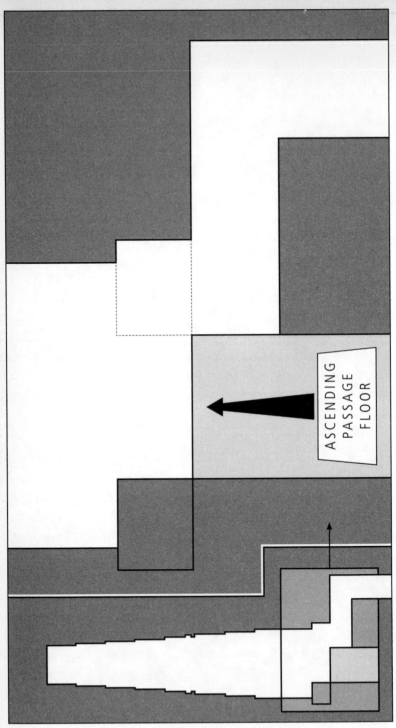

The entry into the Grand Gallery, looking south

showing corbellings, ramps and 'well shaft'

western side, which would have coincided with the entrance to the 'well shaft', is missing, but otherwise there are 28 holes on each side.

The whole structure of the Gallery is corbelled in seven sections, its width gradually narrowing until the top section is once again 41.21 P″ wide. In fact, if the Gallery were 'telescopically collapsed', this section would sit on top of the ramps to form a simple continuation of the ascending passage. Halfway up either side wall, meanwhile, runs a groove that is apparently intended to hold an elevated 'suspended floor'.

At the top end of the Gallery floor, the explorer is confronted after 1812.47832 P″ by the riser of a huge 'step' (the so-called Great Step) 35.763 P″ high, which marks the exact east-west axis of the Pyramid. The south wall, however, is not reached until 68.744 P″ further up the slope, at which point a 'hidden step' 5.3 P″ high is hinted at by the passage geometry and confirmed by the topmost ramp hole (*see diagram page 150*).

The code meaning of all this looks likely to be fairly mind-boggling. But it has to be expressed none the less.

Arrival at 1st April AD 33 along this upper path will bring with it a sudden explosion of illumination sufficient to blast apart all existing restrictions of thought and outlook. Lower and upper consciousness will gradually become fused at the physical level as a new dispensation of suspended enlightenment for humanity is inaugurated, sufficient to survive any over-idealistic initiatives at this time (which will prove utterly fatal) and to bridge over the undermining of the ensuing path between AD 58 and AD 256/296. This dispensation will last until the autumn of 1845, when it will 'come down to earth again' with the inception of a new, balanced level of existence that will have its beginnings between the autumn equinox of 1845 and the summer solstice of 1914. By 1933, consequently, a new era will be in progress.

The fact, of course, that both the front and the back of the Great Step land us squarely on astronomically significant days of the

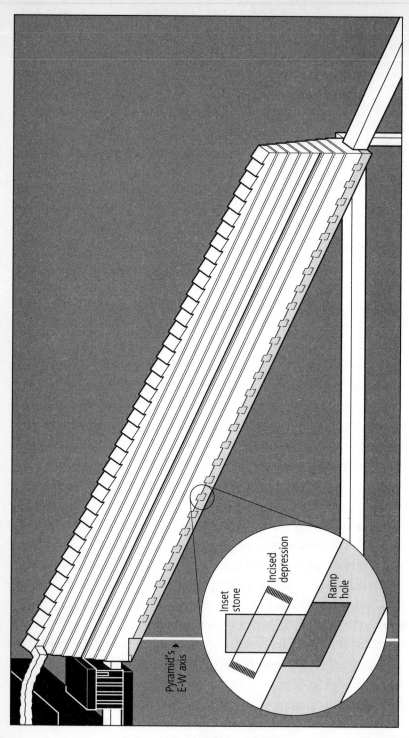

Inset stone

Incised depression

Ramp hole

Pyramid's
E-W axis ►

Projection of the Grand Gallery

122

year offers a powerful hint that our decoding techniques are so far pretty much in tune with the designer's intentions.

Corresponding historical events, meanwhile, are not hard to identify. As a result of the Jesus initiative (and possibly similar contemporary developments, too) a new dimension of awareness does seem to have entered the world early in the first century AD. True, it did not immediately transform human society or behaviour – indeed, those who responded to it too enthusiastically at the time were soon eliminated. Among these we may count not only Jesus himself, but most of his followers, too, much as he himself predicted. Nazorean (i.e. Jewish) Christianity was exterminated, its distant echoes preserved only by the Gnostics, by the Desert Fathers, and eventually in part by Islam. But one form of Christianity did manage to survive. It did so by successfully adapting to conditions as they actually were. This was the Pauline version of Christianity that we still know today. Nevertheless, even this second-hand and apparently Hellenized version of the movement was to have its positive effects. To this day, it continues to underlie much of Western thought, culture, morality and law, and while these have had their nefarious effects, too – not only on the Western psyche itself, but also on other, equally valid cultures overseas – it has also been responsible for much that is good and progressive.

Lest it be thought (as many Pyramidologists think) that the Grand Gallery represents a blanket endorsement of traditional Christianity, however, it needs to be remembered that the dispensation of growing enlightenment that the Gallery represents is clearly depicted as being 'suspended' – at least until the latter half of the 19th century and the beginning of the twentieth. Far from justifying the crass day-to-day activities of any known faith or religion, it hangs in the air above us, overshadowing all our terrestrial activities in ways that are not always obvious. It is a climate of thought, not an everyday creed; a paradigm of growing awareness, not a set of dogmatic, conceptual blinkers. In Christianity, it is perhaps mysticism; in Judaism, Hasidism; in Islam, Sufism; in Buddhism, Zen. Far from imprisoning our minds, it liberates them. Far from preserving us in aspic, it transforms us.

The Great Step, now much damaged

And in this way it prepares us for future possibilities that lie far beyond anything that we can yet imagine...

STARWATCH
TWO

THE HIGHER POWERS HAVE EVIDENTLY INTERVENED. At a precise point during the second millennium BC, humanity has been brought into direct contact either with the Elohim themselves or with some artefact or device that they have left behind, and that is only waiting to be discovered at this time.

Such, at all events, is the apparent message of the granite plug.

Granite, after all, seems specifically to represent the intervention on Earth of higher powers from 'out there'. Indeed, since it is the selfsame red granite as was used to encase the 'Martian' Third Pyramid, there may be some suggestion that the Elohim have previously operated on the Red Planet, too – though not necessarily, of course, that that was where they originated.

In which case it might be thought that they have already left their characteristic 'Orion signature' – duly adjusted for the epoch in question – not merely in the layout of the mighty monuments of Giza, but at some similar site on Mars as well.

Unfortunately, however (as we shall see), Orion is unlikely to have had any signature at all at the time.

But then, what concerns us directly here is in any case not so much ancient Mars as more recent Earth – and more specifically, Earth during the spring of 1453 BC. And the particular question that poses itself is whether the Pyramid's granite plug represents an actual intervention from outside, or merely the activation of some kind of remote, delayed-action device.

Or perhaps we should be thinking in terms not of either/or, but of both/and...

To consider only the case of the Israelite Exodus, there are heavy hints in the biblical account that Moses – who, according to the New Testament at Acts 7:22, had indeed been trained as an Egyptian hierophant – was largely inspired in his epoch-making initiative by the Great Pyramid itself, and notably by the geographical application of its passage angle and the geometry of its constantly moving solar reflections. So, at least, I deduced in my earlier book.[19]

But there are also clear signs in the text of some kind of actual encounter, too. It is not merely a case of vague, passing references that might have been inserted by some latter-day scribe for mere reasons of propaganda. Again and again we are told how Moses, in the course of the great journey, meets some kind of superior entity amid the smoke and clouds of Sinai's holy mountain, how he is there presented with the stone tablets on which the stern demands of his people's new dispensation (not just 10 of them, but all of 613) are inscribed, how he is instructed to place them in a mysterious 'ark', how this in turn is kept well outside the camp in a kind of mobile temple known as the 'tabernacle', and how Moses regularly consults the entity within it while a mysterious column of smoke stands guard outside the entrance. Similar columns of smoke, it seems, guide and protect the Israelites as they pursue the journey to their promised land.

It all seems like some extravagant myth or fairy story. Yet on this occasion something much more real and actual seems to have been involved.

Several points are particularly intriguing:

- *For a start, while the mountain in question is often referred to as 'Sinai', the texts often give it a different name. That name is 'Horeb'. The word comes from Egyptian **Hor'ib**, 'heart of Horus'. But Horus, it will be recalled, is not merely the Egyptian word for 'sky'. It is also the name of one of the mysterious founders themselves – those ancient gods of the beginning who, in the event, are central to our current discussion.*

- *Secondly, Moses' meeting with the entity allegedly takes place amid horrendous thunderings and lightnings on a smoking mount Sinai whose emanations spell death for anybody else who approaches it. The description is typical of a volcano. Yet Sinai has not been volcanic for thousands of years. Evidently, then, the phenomenon – like the strange columns of smoke themselves – is artificial, and presumably reveals the presence of some kind of advanced technology.*

- *Next, the terrifying entity whom Moses meets in the clouds amid the thunderings and lightnings, and which modern texts blandly translate as 'God', is in fact described in the Hebrew as **Elohim** — i.e. 'gods' in the plural – which of course is precisely the term that we have already settled on to represent the ancient founders themselves. This proves nothing, of course, since we ourselves fed the term into the equation in the first place. Nevertheless, the fact is thought-provoking, to say the least.*

- *Finally, the entity insists on concealing its face (Ex.34:18–23). It is also extremely cagey about revealing its true name. Pressed by Moses at Exodus 3:13–16, it offers only the enigmatic **EHYEH ASHER EHYEH** – 'I am what I am', or possibly 'I will be what I will be'. Thereafter, consequently, it is referred to by the texts as **YHWH** (later transcribed as 'Jehovah'), or 'He that is (what he is)'. These seem to be the signs of an entity that is not only in some way terrifyingly superhuman, but can assume any form or identity at will. If a real entity, consequently, it is a very advanced one indeed.*

What the Exodus account describes, then, begs to be seen as the selfsame encounter between humanity and the gods that is predicted by the Great Pyramid via the granite plug at the beginning of its ascending passage. The length of the plug suggests that it is an encounter whose effects will last some 200 years, whether directly or via the mysterious powers of the 'ark' and the tablets stored within it. These are said by the texts to be capable of defying gravity by piling up the waters of the River Jordan, of turning the tide of battles, and of incinerating anybody who so much as touches them. Thereafter, it seems, the contact will cease and the power wane. And indeed, the perceived power of the ark did fade over the centuries until, after being captured and then returned as 'jinxed' by the Philistines, it was turned into a mere ritual object in the temple, before disappearing completely at the time of the Babylonian sack of Jerusalem.

Could it be, then, that the granite plug constitutes not so much a prediction as a promise – a promise on the part of the founding Elohim that they would return at this juncture to inaugurate a new, upward path for humanity? If so, then that path was to be a stern and demanding one. Its burdens (represented both by the great granite blocks and by the heavy stone tablets that the Israelites were supposed to carry with them in their ark wherever they went) would in the end prove too much for humanity to take on its shoulders. The full opening up of the upward path would prove impossible at this time.

Yet the Great Pyramid's ancient designers were obviously good psychologists, too. Having revealed that an upward path was potentially there, they had inevitably kindled vast human interest and curiosity.

What did it entail? What did it promise? What, if anything, lay beyond it?

The result was a valiant attempt to take the upward path as it were by storm. Instead of fully accepting the evolutionary demands – evidently some kind of expansion of consciousness – that was demanded by the Elohim, contemporary humanity determined to gain entrance to it as it were by the back door. In the Great Pyramid, this involved symbolically burrowing around the perceived 'obstruction' and through the Pyramid's softer limestone masonry. Mere ritual acts would, in the event, be substituted for real mental and spiritual evolution.

In historical fact it was the Caliph Al Mamun's workmen who performed the necessary excavations – but it could just as easily have been anybody else.

The required expansion of consciousness did indeed occur – but it would be delayed by nearly 1500 years. Moreover, no further intervention by the Elohim would be involved. Or at least, none was predicted by the Great Pyramid. The sudden explosion of consciousness that evidently occurred with the advent of Jesus of Nazareth was simply the final fruition of a plant of fixed lifespan that had been sown at the time of the Exodus, more or less as Jesus himself was often at pains to point out.

Here, then, as in the subterranean passages, the Pyramid's designers were doing far more than just dating a promise. They were actually predicting the future.

Quite how they managed this is open to question. Possibly they had actually seen it all before. Possibly it is what always happens on any intelligent world – provided, at least, that its civilization lasts long enough. There is a second possibility, though. Possibly the Elohim are capable of creating the future merely through the act of predicting it – the ultimate case, in fact, of self-fulfilling prophecy.

But there is a third possibility, too. It is that the Elohim are lords not only of space, but of time as well – much as the Exodus accounts appear specifically to suggest.

The suggestion may seem mind-boggling. Yet the more they reveal themselves in the Great Pyramid, the less surprising this possibility seems...

13

THE
STRATEGY
OF
STASIS

THE FLOOR OF THE GRAND GALLERY, as we have seen, is symbolically 'undermined' between AD 58 and AD 256/296 by the entrance to the Queen's Chamber passage. The removal of the bridging slab that originally concealed it effectively removes the floor of the Gallery, so preventing any further progress up it. Hence, presumably, the fact that the Gallery's dispensation of enlightenment is represented as being 'suspended'.

There are, it seems, simply no survivors to propagate it.

Some have, of course, already met their fate by turning to the right too soon and so tumbling into the 'well shaft'. They are evidently represented by the real zealots of the time, the religious kamikazes of the first century AD. Perhaps it is significant that the east-west axis of the low passage leading to it seems, on the Queen's Chamber passage timescale, to mark the summer of AD 70, the very date of the final catastrophic elimination of Jewish Christianity with the brutal Roman sacking of Jerusalem.

Others, though, have evidently compromised. Having at least reached the plane of dawning re-integration, they have decided to rest on their laurels, not unreasonably deducing that, since a message needs messengers to proclaim it, their first imperative is survival. They are, as we have seen, the bearers of conventional religion, whether Christian or otherwise.

And it is their path that seems to be symbolized by the Queen's Chamber complex.

This may, of course, seem an improbably narrow interpretation. But then it should be remembered that there were virtually no other idealistic paths to follow at the time.

After the little 3.32 P″ notch or 'peak' that originally secured the lower end of the bridging slab, the Queen's Chamber passage floor leads southwards horizontally for 1282.81285 P″ to a sudden downward step of 20.61 P″. Now 67.5946 P″ high, the 41.21 P″-wide limestone passage, still rectangular in cross section, then continues for a further 216.5668 P″ before entering the Queen's Chamber itself.

Thanks to the step *in mid-passage* and the indeterminate notch at its beginning, the timescale is not easy to determine, but a general reading is nevertheless possible.

On rising just above the level of dawning re-integration, the more evolved terrestrial mortals will choose a path of stasis that will open up from AD 58, thus effectively undermining the topmost path of all. At some point along this path (possibly in or around AD 1228), this slightly overblown path will undergo a 'death' that will take it 'back down to basics' again.

It is interesting to note that the suggested mid-passage dating coincides with the death of St Francis of Assisi, whose life and teachings certainly represented a considerable 'return to basics'. But then he was merely part of a more general movement of enquiry and new idealism that started to make itself felt at around this time. It is less easy to date the chamber itself, however. Apparent code indications of either 2279 or 7276 for its entrance may be misleading. Of more significance may be the positioning of its gable in the Pyramid's side-elevation (*see below*).

The Queen's Chamber itself is 10 RC across and 11 RC from east to west. It is constructed entirely of fairly rough-hewn limestone,

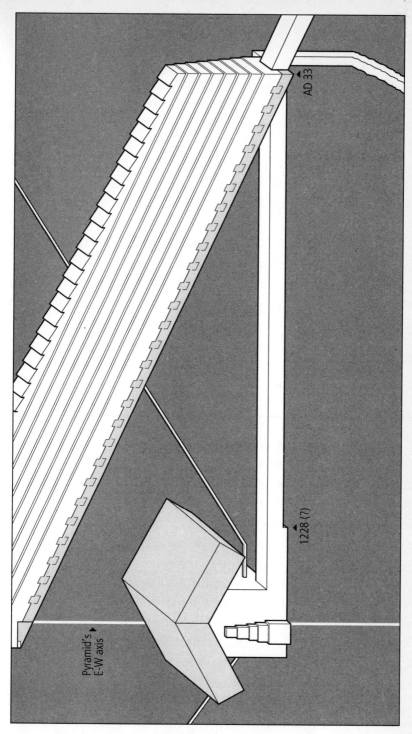

Pyramid's
E-W axis ►

1228 (?) ►

AD 33 ►

Projection of the Queen's Chamber complex

often impregnated with salt, which exudes in crystalline form from the walls. It may once have contained a limestone sarcophagus. Its roof consists of a 12-stone gable, the ridge of its upward-pointing arrowhead exactly on the Pyramid's east-west axis, and thus directly below the riser of the Grand Gallery's 'Great Step' (*see previous chapter*). In its left-hand wall is a five-storeyed niche rising to 184.264 P" (code equivalent of [4 × 35.76 P"] + 2 RC), its axis lying 25 P" beyond that of the chamber itself.

Into the north and south walls run semi-rectangular 'air shafts', whose last 5 P" into the chamber were originally left uncut. These run first horizontally, then upwards towards the Pyramid's north and south faces. The southern shaft continues to within some 25 metres of the south face, then encounters what appears to be a stone portcullis, as yet unopened. The northern shaft carefully skirts the masonry of the Grand Gallery, then appears to continue for a similar distance. According to Bauval *et al*, the meridian orientation of this shaft in around 2500 BC was towards the star Beta Ursae Minoris (*see Chapter 3*) – though the fact that it is diverted around the side of the Grand Gallery may suggest that, for interpretational purposes, it is not to be thought of as targeting any *particular* star or direction. The diversion, after all, is clearly deliberate: merely siting both shafts further west in the chamber would have made it quite unnecessary in the first place.

The meridian orientation of the southern shaft during the same epoch, meanwhile, was directly towards the Dog Star, Sirius (formerly identified with the goddess Isis). Since the code stipulates that movement through time is represented by progress southwards, the northern shaft would thus appear to stand for influences coming into the chamber from outside, while the southern one evidently represents some kind of emergence or escape. *Yet both, as we have seen, are blocked at the outset.*

The final era along this path, which may last for up to a thousand years, is dedicated to the continuing efforts of terrestrial mortals to achieve balance and re-integration in the purely physical context. Were final transcendence to be attained, however, help would be necessary from beyond

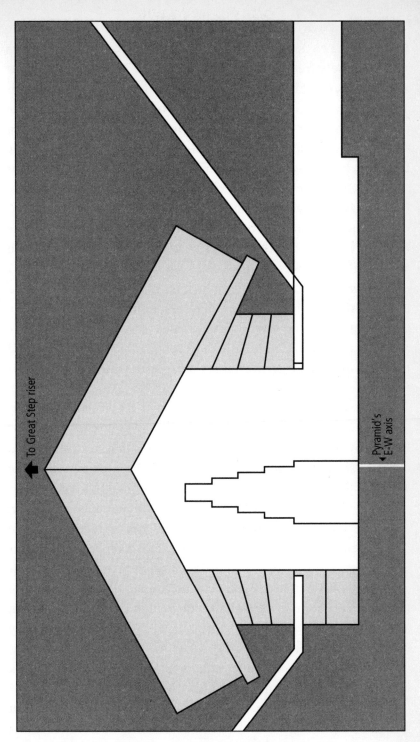

The Queen's Chamber, looking west

Earth, whereupon eventual emergence would ensue, possibly in the direction of the star Sirius. Yet both avenues are effectively blocked. Instead, emergence for those who achieve completion and illumination via this route will depend upon their rejoining the topmost path and providing the physical vehicle for the latter's insights to 'come back down to earth' again from the year 1845 onwards.

Such, then, is evidently the destiny of those (including many Christians) who will continue doggedly to pursue their perceived religious destiny far into the future. This particular path, though, is unlikely to bear cosmological fruit of its own, despite much toil and heartbreak.

The conventionally religious, it seems, will still need to raise their sights and open their minds. Thus far, it is true, the one thing that has saved them has been their adherence to ancestral religious teachings. Eventually, however, they are going to have to see through these to the deeper, unspoken truths that they enshrine.

'For now,' as St Paul put it, 'we see as in a mirror, indistinctly, but then face to face.'

Only by working slowly through their illusions, discarding their conceptual blinkers and (as the upward-pointing gable suggests) adopting the more adventurous and open-minded outlook represented by the topmost path of all will they eventually succeed in transcending Earth and making it to the stars. Indeed, they are destined to be the very bearers of that more advanced form of enlightenment: its survival actually depends on theirs.

Thus it is, then, that the recently-discovered 'portcullis' near the top end of the southern 'air shaft' may represent nothing less than a *gateway to the stars*. The fact that it has been found to be firmly shut, however, tends to confirm that this particular gateway is closed to humanity, and will remain so at least until the destiny represented by the chamber is fulfilled.

So that it would be no surprise at all were it to be found that behind it, in harmony with the five-based symbolism of the rest of the chamber, lie *four others*.

Meanwhile the very idea of an eventual Odyssey across the cosmos may of course seem startling, even if it is apparently blocked. Yet the chamber's 'air shaft' symbolism, as recently unearthed by Bauval and his colleagues, seems to say nothing less.

But then, in the topmost passages and chambers, even more startling developments are by now apparently afoot...

STARWATCH
THREE

THE GODS, IT SEEMS, ARE WAITING. *Far out in the depths of the cosmos, they are ever alert to the remote stirrings of awakening intelligence on those planets on which they have laid their stupendous time traps. They are even prepared to intervene at rare critical moments in order to encourage their inhabitants to realize their full potentialities.*

On Earth, this evidently happened in the northern spring of 1453 BC. For many years the immemorial Elohim made their presence felt. Then they departed again. The silence returned. Yet somewhere down there amid the mountains and deserts, somewhere beside the blue seas and the flashing rivers, something was stirring. The seed that they had planted was germinating, growing, emerging, stretching itself into a mighty tree.

The time would come, they knew, when that tree would bear fruit.

But what kind of a tree would it be? Would the inhabitants of earth tend it and nurture it, or would they mutilate it and misuse it? Would they, perhaps, turn it into a god on its own account, instead of asking where it had come from and what it meant?

Would they determinedly climb the signpost instead of following the road?

There are always such risks. All worlds must follow their own destiny. If they are not allowed to make mistakes, their inhabitants will never learn.

And if they never learn, they will never achieve the degree of evolution without which the ancient tree cannot hope to bear its destined fruit.

Yet those lords of space and time were confident – confident enough even to acknowledge within their prime terrestrial monument that the tradition of growing enlightenment that they had inaugurated would totally die out before even a millennium-and-a-half had run its course.

Or rather, its bearers would.

Yet the seed had been sown. The record of those early achievements would be preserved. And so, in their own good time, those whom their initiative had inspired – however obliquely – would explore and elaborate its insights over the centuries.

In its name they would create divine pantheons, promulgate dogmas, erect rituals, raise mighty temples, found elaborate and self-perpetuating priestly hierarchies. In its name they would produce sublime pieces of art, of sculpture, of music. In its name they would express their understanding in vast tracts of scripture and weighty tomes of theology. And constantly the effort would be to deepen and broaden the original insights, to apply them to the world as it developed, to use them to probe the human soul itself.

And eventually (the Elohim were sure) they would start to rediscover the heart of the matter. It was necessary only that the Terrans – Earth's inhabitants – should persist with their search. Provided that they did, the true sense of the original insights would at last begin to re-emerge from beneath the accumulated verbiage of centuries. Dropping – albeit with great reluctance at first – all the irrelevant ritual paraphernalia, they would lay claim to the ancient inheritance that they had sought for so long to veil behind the dense veils of religion and dogma.

And so, in the event, it was not their religions that would transform them. It was not their religions that would bring them to perfection. It was not their religions that would liberate them. Their religions would merely bind them closer to Earth.

Yet at the same time those religions would prepare the ground. Thanks to them, the ancient tree of the Prime Initiative, so long neglected, would at last start to bear fruit.

The Great Pyramid's chronograph times the process. It has already been going on now for a good century-and-a-half. It is still going on now, at this *very moment. Already the truth – as yet barely recognized, still less generally taken seriously – is starting to stare humanity full in the face.*

The truth that will set us free.

14

TRANSCENDING EARTH

THE 'GREAT STEP' AT THE TOP END OF THE GRAND GALLERY marks the entrance to the astonishing King's Chamber complex. Although its riser (marking the centreline of the Pyramid) fixes the autumn equinox of 1845, and its back edge (on the floorline scale) pinpoints 22 June 1914, the scale-change effect of the step is actually to re-date the entrance of the complex to 20 November 1933 – whereupon projecting the original floorline further appears to mark out the advent of some kind of 'anti-illumination' or 'anti-transformer' between this date and 10 August 1944.

Between the autumn of 1845 and the summer of 1914 the lofty insights spawned during the first century AD will have their eventual results as they 'come back down to earth again' and find flesh-and-blood humans to host them. Corresponding 'anti-insights' will also resurface, however.

The period in question may at first sight seem to have been fairly unremarkable – too late for the industrial revolution, too early for the atomic and space ages. Yet it in fact marked the dawning of what might be called the Age of the Human Imagination. This was to be an age whose prophets, unlike those of the Renaissance before it, would look not to the past, but fearlessly to the future. True, there had been earlier visionaries such as Roger Bacon and Leonardo da Vinci, but they had been mere flashes in the darkness, largely unremarked by their contemporaries. Da Vinci had even written in code.

Now, however, thanks to the efforts of Faraday and Morse, Maxwell and Edison, Hertz and Marconi, Mach and Einstein – all of them men who dared to think the unthinkable – the idea at last arose that humanity could not merely emulate the ancients, but actually beat them hollow. The great science-fictionists from Verne and Wells to Asimov and Clarke, even less hidebound by immediate practicalities, took up the Great Idea, elaborated it and pushed it even further. Then the technologists in turn set about turning those imaginings into hard realities – from the submarine to the tank, from the self-propelled vehicle to the heavier-than-air flying machine, from the space rocket to the communications satellite, from actual lunar landings to orbiting space stations. As a result, we now scarcely bat an eyelid as we fund hugely expensive organizations such as NASA and the European Space Agency in deference to such dreams – dreams that only a few decades ago would have been regarded as quite laughable. At the same time, the non-technical laity are becoming ever more deeply seduced by mind-stretching television series such as *Star Trek*, just as their grandfathers before them were inspired to become founding space engineers by mere strip-cartoon characters of the stamp of Dan Dare in the *Eagle*. The whole thing, in fact, is steadily acquiring an almost religious dimension – always a sure sign that the original Prime Initiative is being in some way touched upon, in however tangential a form.

For the unspoken conviction that underlay all this from the beginning was itself almost religious in character: *that the human race can achieve absolutely anything that it can set its mind to.*

With the final birth of that idea some century-and-a-half ago, the prison doors were at last flung open, the spell of self-limitation finally broken. From railways to telegraph, from telephone to radio and television, from the wonders of science to the imponderabilities

Key:
- Tura limestone
- Local limestone
- Red granite

3989   2989 2949   1999
1845

Pyramid's
E-W axis ▸

The King's Chamber passage era is entered via the 'Great Step'

of relativity, from the atomic age to the information revolution, from the adventure of flight to the romance of space, humanity was set on an exponential development curve whose far end could not even be guessed at, even if it had one.

The sole limitation was the human mind: the sole frontier was the frontier of the human imagination. And those who were unprepared to cross it – the traditionalists, the technophobes, the neophobes – were destined to be forever left behind.

Yet the idea was not a new one. Rather than a birth, it was a re-birth. True to the Great Pyramid's blueprint, it went back directly to the first century AD. 'If you have no more faith than a mustard seed,' Jesus had told his followers at Matthew 17:20, 'you will tell this mountain "Move over", and it will move: nothing will be beyond your capabilities.' All that was required, it seems, was that the human mind be aligned with the larger, cosmic will – the sovereignty of the spirit, the kingdom of heaven.

And now, at last, it was all starting to come true.

The Great Pyramid proceeds to map out the consequences (*see diagram overleaf*). A low, horizontal, limestone passage now leads further southward into the Pyramid. It is 41.21 P" square in cross section and 52.02874 P" long. It lies atop the 50th course of masonry and 153 courses below the summit platform. Its significance is therefore clear.

Terrestrial mortals on the topmost path will now enter a new dispensation dedicated to a perfecting process that will provide the basis for eventual earthly enlightenment. Its initial stage, however, will involve a 'bending low': this will start in late 1933 and terminate on 30 November 1985.

True enough, the brief period in question does not itself come across as particularly enlightened. It encompassed not only the rise of Hitler (perhaps specifically foreshadowed, if rather less accurately than usual, in the 'hidden step'), but also the Jewish holocaust, the Second World War, Josef Stalin, Korea, Vietnam, Pol Pot, Saddam Hussein and plagues and natural disasters without number.

But then the symbolism is careful *not* to label the new dispensation as already enlightened. It is 'an age of completion and perfection' designed to *lead* to eventual enlightenment. And for that, it seems, some nasty shocks are necessary first.

In order to enter and know the light, in fact, it is first essential that we get to know our darkness – all those aspects of ourselves that we traditionally push as far from us as possible, often by projecting them on to others. Thus rejected, they become our self-created Shadow and, thus unrecognized, their power to waylay and harm us is vastly increased – which was why the great Swiss psychologist Carl Gustav Jung always insisted that the process of making the unconscious conscious and deliberately *withdrawing* our projections is literally so vital for our survival.

We have, in short, to learn to become who we are, rather than who we wish we were. We have to make even the darkness light. And it is the King's Chamber initiative that is designed above all to foster that process.

Thus it is that the Antechamber proper commences in late November, 1985. From the start its roof is made of *granite*, even though its floor and walls continue for a while to be of limestone. The width of the passage continues to be 41.21 P″, but in its upper part it broadens out in stages to 62.256 P″, the left-hand wainscot being 5 RC high and the right-hand one 7.77 P″ higher. After 13.2243 P″ the limestone floor changes abruptly to granite, and 7.3793 P″ later the wainscots follow suit, at least in their upper portions. The lower portions in due course do likewise, first on the right and then on the left.

And so the marvellous mathematics begin. The total height of the chamber, at 149.44071 P″, is an exact one-hundredth of the sum of the full-design Pyramid's height and base length. Its length is 116.26025 P″ – which is of course 356.24235 P″ divided by π. Its southern end thus marks 21 February 2499. At this point, its southern granite wall (*see illustration page 44*) is divided by four strange, rectangular grooves, each terminating at the bottom in a kind of 'scoop', and leading upwards some 96 P″ (8 × 12 P″) to where the top 12 P″ of wall suddenly reverts to limestone. Nothing could be clearer, then, than that physical humanity must by this point be ready finally to leave Earth behind and undertake a non-terrestrial

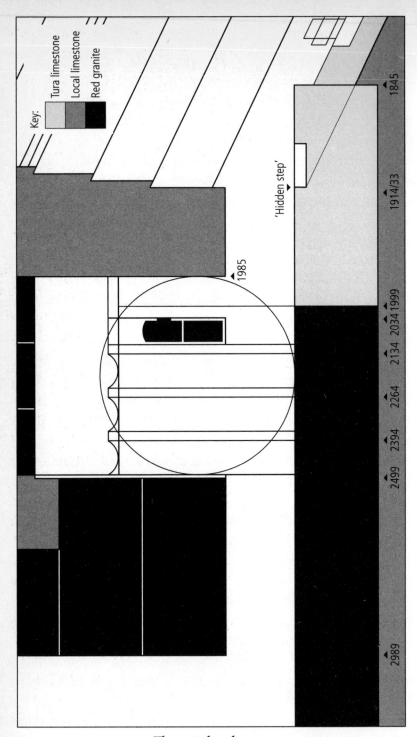

Key:
- Tura limestone
- Local limestone
- Red granite

'Hidden step'

1845
1914/33
2034 1999
2134
2264
2394
2499
2989

1985

The antechamber era

Circumference of superimposed circle measures 365.242 P″

150

journey to a higher and more advanced world – a journey into the cosmos, no less.

In side elevation, meanwhile, the east wainscot, at 5 RC high, marks out with the 5-RC-long granite floor a square whose area is 25 square Royal Cubits – an exact quarter of the ancient Egyptian unit of area, the *aroura*. Yet the largest circle that can be described within the same side elevation has a diameter of 116.26025 P", and thus a circumference of 365.24235 P" (*see diagram opposite*): consequently *it, too*, has an area of one quarter-*aroura*.[19] Thus, not only is the circle successfully squared – a theoretically impossible feat in itself – but the direct mathematical relationship is defined between the Royal Cubit, whose existence Egyptologists readily acknowledge, and the Sacred Cubit, whose existence they routinely deny.

And meanwhile earth, space and time are shown to be at last in total harmony.

By 30 November 1985 terrestrial life will be increasingly overshadowed by non-terrestrial concerns, and by 21 February 1999 will have succeeded in setting foot permanently in space. By the end of this era, during which Earth, space and time will finally have been brought into harmony, humanity will have advanced to the point where it is ready finally to leave Earth for other, more advanced physical worlds. This must occur by 21 February 2499.

Thus far, events seem more or less to fit. At the very moment represented by the beginning of the chamber, after all, the imminent approach of Halley's Comet was prompting the dispatch of no less than five space probes to meet and examine it. Of these the European Space Agency's *Giotto* managed to get closest (some 605 km) on 13–14 March 1986. Yet even today the true nature of this strange, alien body has not been fully determined.

By then, however, humanity had already succeeded in at last getting one foot semi-permanently into space. On 20 February the Soviet Union had succeeded in launching *Mir*, the world's first permanent manned space station. That station is still there – just – at the time of writing. But in due course (perhaps by early 1999, the date apparently laid down for humanity's definitive colonization of space by the granite flooring of the Pyramid's antechamber) it will be joined by another – the even more permanent International Space Station, designed to serve as a jumping-off point for destinations much further out in the cosmos, and in itself symbolic of an emergent coming-together of human consciousness.

And so a greater humanity will finally have got *both* feet into space.

As for the final date in the antechamber (21 February 2499) this is of course extraordinarily close to that of the ancient Egyptian 'Last Time', as calculated astronomically by Bauval *et al* (*see Chapter 3*) – the date when the Earth's slow, precessional cycle will finally bring the constellation Orion to its highest point on the meridian. But then, while the Pyramidal date is exact, the astronomical one is only approximate. *There can be little doubt, in fact, that the two dates are for all practical purposes one and the same.*

The Last Time, then – the time when Orion finally reaches his culmination in the firmament – is truly significant. It marks the date by which humanity must finally have transcended Earth. And the reason is clear. Far down below, in the subterranean complex (*see Chapter 11*), something truly disturbing is about to happen.

Within 70 years, human life on Earth is set to be extinguished.

The precise reason is not spelt out. Perhaps it will simply be one of the inevitable geological or meteorological results of the Earth's gradual precession. Perhaps something more catastrophic is about to occur – a major nuclear disaster, a shifting of the poles caused by imbalances in the polar icecaps, even a meteoric or asteroidal impact. The modern French seer Mario de Sabato[19] suggests the first, the Flem-Aths[11] the second, Nostradamus[21] apparently the third.

Whatever the reason, disaster looms for earthbound humanity. There can be no question, of course, of transporting the whole population of Earth to another planet. And yet, if the human race is to survive, *some* of its inhabitants must be saved.

The process of selection may be less difficult than one might expect. In all probability most people – the familiar traditionalists, the technophobes, the neophobes – will simply refuse to believe in the necessity for such a 'Noah's ark' operation in the first place.

They would 'rather bear the ills they have than fly to others that they know not of'. Those who leave, consequently, will be largely self-chosen, committed to a huge leap of faith that most others will regard as sheer folly, if not actual suicide.

But what on earth will have prompted that leap in the first place? How will even the pioneers have come to believe in the necessity for such a venture? More to the point, what is it that will have prepared them, equipped them and shown them where to go?

Once again, it is in the Antechamber that the answer gradually swims into view.

STARWATCH
FOUR

DOWN ON THE PLANET'S SURFACE, *things were stirring. Where formerly life had remained fairly static, now greater and greater numbers of Earth's inhabitants were starting to travel. Soon the fever of movement was becoming a frenzy. Millions surged to and fro almost daily in a rising tide of apparent agitation.*

Before long, that frenzy acquired a vertical dimension, too. Shining cylinders of life started to skim through the atmosphere, binding far continents and cities together. Then experimental craft began to explore near space itself. Huge fire machines hurled larger and larger craft into orbit. Sitting precariously atop them, humans made it to the moon and back. Smaller probes headed far out from Earth, first towards the planets, then towards the sun, and finally into deep space itself. Some of them even bore messages to the unknown inhabitants of other worlds.

And eventually Earth's inhabitants began to make space itself their home.

But other things were happening, too. Electronic messages were starting to crackle to and fro – first along wires, then directly through the atmosphere. Some were reflected naturally back down to Earth again, others spilled far out into the cosmos. Soon other transmissions were being beamed up to reflectors in synchronous orbit, then back down again to the seething surface.

The planet was gradually weaving a nervous system of its own.

And now the target changed. New transmissions were deliberately beamed up deep into space – transmissions designed to alert others to Earth's new awakening and imminent emergence. Those transmissions were intercepted.

But then the Elohim were in any case perfectly well aware of what was happening. They, after all, had planned and timed it in the first place. Down there on the surface their ancient monuments of witness still stood. One day, perhaps, in their own good time, the inhabitants of Earth would succeed in understanding them. And at that point their almost explosive emergence would become less chaotic and unplanned. Instead, it would become focused and controlled.

Humanity would at last know where it was going.

Not – it has to be said – in a technical and 'outward' direction only. For the 'inner' world, too, would be in a ferment of change. Humanity's spiritual, psychological and mental evolution would all be unfolding at unprecedented rates. Some Terrans, indeed, aghast at the sheer multi-dimensionality of what was seemingly happening, would withdraw into their shells and convince themselves that the familiar world of spirituality alone would suffice to fulfil their ultimate destiny, and that little or no 'outer' effort would therefore be necessary. Brainwork must be belittled, technology shunned like the Plague.

In reality, of course, the inner can no more progress without the outer than the outer can progress without the inner. True, some highly evolved souls – Earth's great sages and teachers – might sometimes claim to have achieved inner union with the infinite, albeit at the risk of being accused of delusions of grandeur. But, self-evidently, outer union remains as elusive as ever. They remain the same eccentric and sometimes cantankerous men, the same domineering and sometimes self-obsessed women. Lesser souls generally fare even worse, demonstrating to all except themselves that the entire enterprise has merely been a way of boosting the ego without seeming to – and that the effort to achieve personal *union with the Infinite was always necessarily a contradiction in terms in the first place.*

The only thing that can be the Immensity is the Immensity: the only thing that can be the All is the All.

Hence the present exercise. Sentient life throughout the universe must learn to re-identify itself with the All of which it was in reality always the highest expression. But in order to become greater than he or she currently feels himself or herself to be, a single human being has first to learn to identify with family or friends. Later, that identity has to expand to group, then to tribe or nation. But each step can be achieved only by going a further step beyond it. Tribe must fight tribe, nation must speak peace unto nation.

Thus, in order fully to identify with Earth and with humanity as a whole, it is necessary for humans en masse *to go beyond it and look back on it from space. This was what the almost magical combination of television and the Apollo moon missions managed between them to achieve in the 1960s. Earth-consciousness and ecology duly burgeoned worldwide – and, moreover, for the first time. But if it is to identify with the solar system, humanity will have to go beyond even that, too.*

And so it is that, for the mass of human beings, full cosmic consciousness will be achieved only when humanity reaches the furthest borders of the universe – if, indeed, it has any – and union with the All only when even the All is transcended. Which presumably is why humanity seems to be programmed to set out precisely in that direction.

The great venture into space, in other words, is a sine qua non.

The Elohim have been aware of this since the beginning. They always knew where humanity was going. That was why they encoded it into their mightiest monument of all, before departing again for the stars. Sooner or later humans would realize it and follow.

And still the Elohim are waiting.

But such things cannot be left merely to chance. Stone monuments, like any message, can be misunderstood. Sooner or later actual contact must be arranged. First, simple electronic messages must be exchanged. Earth must be gradually acclimatized to the realization that it is not alone. Any early feelings of threat and alienation must be carefully avoided, or if necessary overcome. But then the great encounter must take place.

The gods must walk on Earth once more.

15

GREAT ENCOUNTERS

AT A POINT JUST 7.3793 P″ BEYOND THE BEGINNING OF THE GRANITE FLOOR, and one Royal Cubit beyond the antechamber's north wall, the 41.21 P″-wide passage through it is suddenly over-shadowed by a portcullis composed of two granite slabs (*compare diagram on page 50*). On the new, granite floor-scale of 1 *n* per year, the date is 14 December 2034.

But the portcullis, paradoxically, does not reach the floor. *Nor could it, having been built into the masonry on either side of the passage.*

At this particular point, moreover, all that actually appears as yet is a kind of 'boss' on its north face. Shaped like the Egyptian hieroglyph for 'bread' (*see diagram page 44*), it has been left proud (like the portcullis's side-rebates) as a result of the builders' having planed down the rest of the face to the extent of 1 P″. The boss is thus 1 P″ thick. Its centre lies 1 P″ to the right of the centre of the slab on which it sits, as well as 1 Sacred Cubit from the latter's eastern end where it is embedded in the left-hand wall. The bottom of its base comes some 5 P″ above the horizontal joint between the two slabs, while the bottom edge of its surface comes some 33.5 P″ above the bottom of the lower slab – which in turn lies just 41.21 P″ above the floor. Clearly, then, the portcullis is marked out as representing a transforming super-mortal bringing illumination and oneness to a troubled Earth.

The top of the portcullis, meanwhile, is rough and irregular. Unless it has been mutilated in antiquity, it looks suspiciously as if it is meant to be seen as having been 'broken off from above'.

Whether appropriately or not, the familiar expression 'bread from heaven' springs to mind.

The dressed-down thickness of the portcullis is 15.75 P″ – which means that its southern face marks a notional date of 28 March 2116. 3.75 P″ further on come a pair of grooves in the wall, each roughly 3.25 P″ deep and 21.5 P″ across, evidently intended for a further portcullis (the available measurements at this point are somewhat less precise than usual). Its symbolic dates are thus fixed at roughly mid–2134 to late 2238. This time, moreover, the grooves descend all the way to the floor. Indeed, they actually extend some 3 P″ below it. At the top, meanwhile, the left-hand groove-extremity is straight, while its right-hand equivalent is carefully sculpted into a semicircular hollow (*see diagrams below and on page 150*).

This arrangement has prompted a plethora of helpful theories designed to explain how it once facilitated the raising and lowering of the now-missing portcullis. Unfortunately, none of them works in practice. But then possibly the portcullis was never there in practice, either.

Two further portcullises of similar size and spacing are then signalled. The symbolic dating for the first is thus from midsummer 2264 to the autumn of 2368, while that for the second is from midsummer 2394 to late 2498 or early 2499. In fact, the latter's terminal date can be timed even more precisely because it coincides with the far south wall of the antechamber, whose position is much more finely known.

And this marks 21 February 2499.

On the basis of symbolic parallels in the biblical Noah-story I originally surmised that the three missing portcullises might have been envisaged as being of limestone.[19] On the other hand, this is

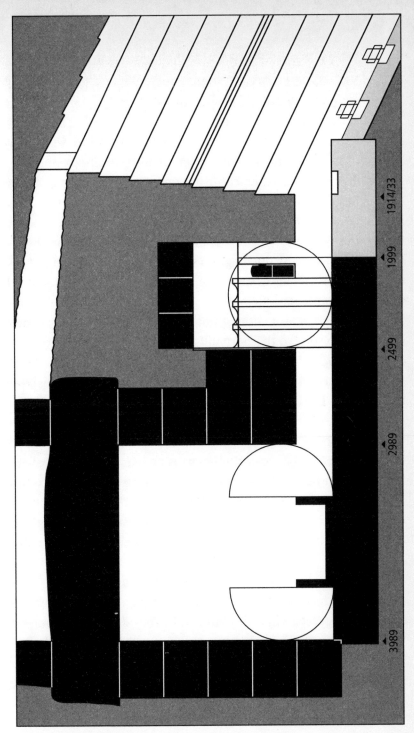

Side-elevation of the King's Chamber complex, looking west
Circumference of each superimposed circle measures 365.242 P"

almost never the case. The much harder granite is a much more suitable material. In this case, then, we are evidently in the presence of not one, but four non-terrestrial visitors – or missions – to Earth. Everything about them proclaims the fact – even the semicircular extremities of the western grooves, apparently signifying the irruption of non-terrestrial influences into the affairs of Earth.

Indeed, there is further confirmation. Seen in side-elevation, the northern 'air shaft' of the King's Chamber spears its way into the chamber *directly through the centrelines of the four portcullises in question (see diagram page 176)*. There is nothing architecturally inevitable about this. As the diagram shows, the long horizontal portion of the shaft seems to have been designed quite deliberately to achieve this particular effect. Since, then, *northern* shafts are by definition for ingress, not egress ('time' in the Pyramid always works from north to south), the portcullises are seen once again to symbolize *incoming* influences and/or life forms.

Between 2034 and 2499, four successive non-terrestrial missions to Earth will take place. Their object will be to transform and perfect the very basis of terrestrial life, to the point where its advanced bearers will be ready to leave Earth and set sail across the cosmos at least 70 years before the next great global extinction. Although the first mission will not fully integrate with life on Earth, the last three will descend fully into mortality, successively closing behind them all regressive options until the only route lies forward.

The evident non-integration of the first incoming mission – the very obvious fact that it fails to reach the floor – is an intriguing feature. It suggests, after all, either that the Elohim will judge it advisable to remain initially at a safe distance, or that their first approach will be actively resisted. At *Century* II.45 the celebrated French seer Michel Nostradamus seems specifically to suggest the latter. In my previously published translation[21] this reads:

The southern end of the antechamber

Too much high heaven the Androgyne bewails,
New-born aloft the sky where blood is sprayed.
Too late that death a mighty race avails.
Sooner or later comes the hoped-for aid.

Piatkus Books

In this case, the term 'Androgyne' – i.e. 'male/female being' – is intriguing, to say the least.

But the same source also suggests that the 'gods', once arrived, will remain until *well after* the final destruction has begun, when what appears to be some kind of 'nuclear winter' will be in progress. At *Century* I.91 he writes:

The gods to men shall make it fully clear
How of the mighty war they'll be the source.
Before the sky shall clear shall sword and spear
To leftward turn with even greater force.

Piatkus Books

So that, even at VI.5, the incomers are still keeping the planet warily under surveillance:

A wave of plague shall bring so great a dearth
While ceaseless rains the Arctic Pole shall sweep:
Samarobryn, a hundred leagues from Earth,
Law-free themselves from politics shall keep.

Piatkus Books

Here the *plural* term 'Samarobryn' is a curious one. Some have seen in it a combination of the Russian words *samo* ('self') and *robotnik* ('worker'). More probably, it is based simply on the word *Samarobriva*, the ancient Celtic name for the French city of Amiens. Possibly Nostradamus is playing, via *Amiens*, on the word *amiantins*, 'the Undefined/Incorruptible Ones' (from the Greek *amiantos*) – which would be highly appropriate. The most striking point, however, is the suggested distance from Earth: 'a hundred leagues' is equivalent to 444.8 kilometres, or 276.4 miles – *almost exactly the orbital altitude of the former American Skylab.*

What, then, is the initial problem likely to be? The most likely candidate seems to be some kind of planetary xenophobia. This, after all, has been more than amply encouraged during recent decades by a positive cascade of books, films and videos portraying possible future incomers from space as rampaging aliens bent on destroying our planet. The archetypal production in this genre was of course H. G. Wells's *War of the Worlds*, of which Orson Welles's celebrated radio production managed to cause such panic all across America in the 1930s. As yet, more balanced series such as the ubiquitous and much-loved *Star Trek* have only partially succeeded in repairing the damage, largely because they are only too prone to suffer intermittently from it themselves. Almost the only entirely benevolent force in the universe, it often seems, is that thinly-disguised version of American mother-and-apple-pie known as the United Federation of Planets. And all the while such attitudes persist, the initial prospects for the coming Great Encounter remain regrettably slim.

Much, clearly, has to do with expectation. As at least one *Star Trek* episode did manage to recognize, the best way of avoiding such cosmic xenophobia is carefully to tie in the features of your arrival with existing planetary beliefs regarding the future advent of benevolent beings from the sky. On Earth, certainly, such beliefs are almost universal.

But then, as we have seen, this fact may originally be due to the Prime Initiative itself.

Thus, the best way for such an advent to be widely welcomed on Earth would be for the incomers to conform to the manner, timing *and even the appearance* of the Messianic return, as long expected by the religious who have preserved the ancient tradition. Since the Elohim seem to be capable of varying and controlling their appearance at will, this ought to pose no problem. In this way Jews, Christians and Muslims would alike have their expectations confirmed: the Awaited Saviour would descend from the clouds arrayed in robes of glory and, wielding positively magical powers, set up his everlasting kingdom on Mount Zion. Then he would send out his 'angels' (i.e. his messengers) to gather together his chosen from all corners of the planet to inherit a new world entirely – a heavenly kingdom, or sky dispensation, that would never pass away.

The general parameters of the archetypical mission certainly accord astonishingly exactly with those long since laid down in the Great Pyramid's enduring stone.

The Elohim, in short, must either incarnate the Messiah in person, or visibly 'take over' a pre-existing human being. He must be no self-deluded megalomaniac, but manifestly their sanctioned vehicle. He must appear in Palestine, sport a beard and long hair, wear flowing robes, speak Aramaic and Hebrew and set up his headquarters in Jerusalem. The Terrans will permit nothing less. In accordance with long tradition – though not with likely historical fact – he must even be white-skinned. As a result, he will be seen either as a living blasphemy or as the Messiah in person – just as, in his day, Jesus himself was.

It is even possible – *just* possible – that he will actually *be* the Messiah. Perhaps it is in reality *his* advent that the biblical prophets always dimly glimpsed. True, it is always challenging to face the actualization of your ideals. It is almost as if ideals were really reserved for 'up there', not 'down here'. Certainly this fundamental clash was something that Jesus's own contemporaries found particularly hard to stomach – and especially the more religious of them.

So that if, in case of the Elohim, the unedifying experience is repeated, it will be no surprise.

But there are other Messianic traditions, too, and all of them will need to be satisfied if the initiative's effects are to be as universal as they will need to be. The new overlord will need, for example, to embody the long-awaited Buddha Maitreya and the traditions associated with him. Nor should the venerable traditions of Hinduism – perhaps the most ancient high religion in the world – be ignored. He will need to be the very incarnation of Kalki, the last and greatest of the avatars of Vishnu.

But then, it seems, he is set to do that anyway.

For Kalki's role will indeed be to bring to an end the current 'Age of Iron' and inaugurate the re-absorption of humanity and the world that it inhabits into the primal Absolute. A positive giant, he will wield *a fiery sword like a comet* as the instrument of his office. And, even more to the point (as we shall see), he will have *a horse's head...*

According to the symbolic features of the antechamber, however, there will be not merely one Messiah, but several. Evidently this is not so much a prediction as a promise. Jews, Christians and Muslims will no doubt be suitably surprised. Nevertheless, there it stands in solid stone.

Presumably, then, this veritable succession of other-worldly beings has a purpose. It is not merely some kind of ritual advent, designed to impress the religious. There is deadly serious business to be done. And indeed, according to the remarkable modern French seer Mario de Sabato,[19, 36] the visitors will have a truly vital task to perform. It will be no mere moral crusade. Their role will not be to separate the righteous from the unrighteous – even though the effect of their initiative may well be to separate those who are prepared to leave Earth from those who are not. Finally resolve our religious and metaphysical problems as they may, they will certainly resolve our scientific and technological ones, too. Emissaries from a part of the universe that will already have achieved its final flowering of consciousness, they will bring with them vast knowledge and almost unbelievable technologies. Thanks to their patient efforts, humanity will advance by several centuries in as many years.

It will need to. For time, evidently, is growing short. A major planetary extinction looms.

As a result, we are going to need to learn new skills – and especially the skills of deep space travel. There will be an urgent need to develop sustainable life-support systems and protected, self-contained travelling environments capable of lasting not merely for years, but perhaps even for generations. Sophisticated techniques of interstellar navigation, possibly at faster-than-light speeds, will be essential – notwithstanding the fact that such speeds are currently supposed to be impossible.

Such is the evident magnitude of the task ahead and the scale of the quantum leap of understanding that will be involved.

And above all, we are going to need to develop the long-mooted spacedrive.

Science fiction this may sound, but circumstances seem likely to force us to turn it into space fact. Possibly the new propulsion-system will take the form of a warp-drive involving the actual deformation of spacetime around the ship. Almost certainly it will involve some form of gravity control. Both may seem highly speculative at present, if not pure fantasy. Yet there is virtually universal agreement among today's major seers that such a drive will indeed be developed. Crossing the cosmos, they insist, will eventually become as easy as crossing Earth's oceans.

Once again, it will need to be. For, as we shall go on to see, the distances involved are likely to be truly vast.

But could not humanity have made it on its own? Even given that time is limited for what may be astronomical reasons, was it always inevitable that help would eventually have to come from 'outside'?

The answer is probably 'No'.

The Greeks, in the person of Hero of Alexandria, were already successfully using a combination of steam power and jet propulsion by around the second century of our era, even if as yet only (as some believe) for opening and closing temple doors. Had not the heavy, stultifying hand of imperial Rome descended on them and choked off all further progress, Renaissance science might have taken wing a thousand years earlier than it did, the industrial revolution might have taken place by the time of Alfred the Great, and man might have been walking on the moon before the Norman conquest.

Incredible the idea may now seem, yet there is absolutely no *a priori* reason why this should not have come to pass.

But then this is not the only possible great might-have-been. Some of the late dinosaurs were not only warm-blooded and bipedal: they had stereo vision, prehensile hands and large brains, and were probably a good deal more intelligent than their contemporaries that were our own humble, shrew-like ancestors. Had the dinosaurs not been almost totally wiped out by their own Terminal Event some 65 million years ago, it is quite possible that they would have made it to the moon long aeons before us, and certainly *some millions of years* before the Greeks...

But this, likewise, was not to be. In the event, only the birds remain, charming the air around us with their songs. And, as a number of human experimental volunteers have discovered, big brains do not necessarily go with feathered flight.

The Elohim, of course, presumably knew all about the dinosaurs at the time when they inaugurated their great Prime Initiative all those thousands of years ago. But that the Greeks, similarly, would in due course fail to make the grade was evidently something that they had to anticipate. It was simply part of the future that they foresaw for humanity and duly depicted in the architecture of their premier monument on Earth. In which case, the Greek initiative may well be one of those that the Great Pyramid depicts as being temporarily 'suspended' during the Grand Gallery era. Possibly it, like its Hebrew counterpart, had its roots in ancient times when the contemporary Myceneans, too, had a traumatic encounter on their own sacred mountain – in this case Mount Olympus – with Zeus, their own 'sky father'. Even if no specific code of laws resulted at the time, possibly the seeds were then sown of as yet unimagined possibilities – seeds which continued for centuries to germinate within the fertile Greek mind until the time of Hero. And possibly that initiative, too, was destined to 'come back down to earth again' only in the mid–19th century of our own era.

If so, it would be appropriate. For the period in question indeed turned out to be *specifically the age of steam.*

The antechamber initiative to which that age led directly was therefore very much a last chance effort, at least for current life on Earth. If humanity was not to go the way of the dinosaurs, Orion must come again. Osiris must be resurrected. The rescuing Messiahs must walk the Earth once more.

STARWATCH
FIVE

STANDING OFF FROM EARTH, the gods look down. It is the selfsame planet that they first visited long before. But in those days it was the planet of **Zep Tepi**, *the First Time. That was the era of Orion's beginnings, the birth of his cycle. For Earth, similarly, it was a time for new beginnings. Newly emerged from under the ice, the northern lands were gradually coming back to life again. The vast prairies were burgeoning, the valleys filling with trees, the mountains loud with insects and birds. And there at the centre of the world's landmass a vast monument field was taking shape.*

Rising beside the Nile – the terrestrial equivalent of the Milky Way – were three huge pyramids, set out in the pattern of the stars of Orion's belt. And, guarding them, a mighty sphinx in the shape of Leo, the celestial Lion.

Their very size would ensure two things. The first was that they would survive. The second was that they would be noticed. And the combination of the two would ensure that, at some distant point in the future, humanity's curiosity would get the better of it.

The site would be explored. The geometry would be deciphered. The message would be decoded.

In due course, that message would duly get through. The realization would dawn that humanity has a destiny, and one that will long outlive Earth. True, the realization would be mythologized, ritualized and turned into mere religious dogma. When the time came for such dogmas to be dismissed, consequently, the message would be dismissed with them. And yet the new realism would breed a new attitude. Humanity would look again.

And there the message would still be, still encoded in enduring stone.

The time, it said, would come for strange encounters, and after that for a great and even stranger departure.

And now, it seems, that time has come.

Yet who welcomes such news? Everyday life may not always be pleasant, but at least it is familiar. To be told that you must leave it or die is never nice. To be told it by mighty, alien beings whom you barely understand is positively unsettling. To let yourself be ruled by them is quite beyond the pale. To be advised that all this must involve changing not merely your home, but your very nature is, frankly, all but unacceptable.

The Elohim are well aware of this.

And so diplomacy has to be the new watchword – and extremely careful diplomacy, at that. The natives, for all their rapidly advancing technology, still have set minds, primitive drives – and sharp teeth. Everything, then, must accord with Earth's expectations. If the doctor is to supply the medicine, the patient must be allowed to specify the shape of the bottle.

There is no place for brutality.

And so the Messiah must come, as predicted, in the clouds of heaven, with great power and glory. And then so must the next, and the next, and the next.

For the final time of Orion, the triumphant harvest time of Earth, is at hand.

16

THE
GATE
OF
HEAVEN

WITH THE FINAL CLOSING OF THE ANTECHAMBER, the portcullises are down. There is no turning back. From now on humanity's path lies unremittingly forward.

And it leads initially through the low, final section of the King's Chamber passage.

Square in cross section, this last horizontal corridor is 41.21 P" wide and high. Unlike the original part of the passage, however, it now passes entirely through granite. Still built on the Pyramid's 50th course of masonry, and thus 153 courses below its summit platform, it is 101.04629 P" long. In combination with the earlier portion, therefore, the total length of the two low corridors itself works out at 153.07503 P" (code equivalent: 153). The symbolic dating for the final entry into the King's Chamber is thus 2nd July 2989. Just to the west, meanwhile, the last, horizontal stretch of the King's Chamber's northern 'air shaft' runs directly in parallel (*see diagram page 176*).

The route towards final enlightenment for terrestrial mortals is now an accompanied one that lies unremittingly forward through a non-terrestrial environment for 490 years.

In short, the great Space Odyssey will have begun – and it will be undertaken *in the company of the Elohim themselves*. We shall be looking at the detailed implications in due course.

Meanwhile the upper path has reached its climax with the final entry into the King's Chamber. Built entirely of granite, this is a positive Aladdin's cave of brilliant mathematics. Not only do the walls consist of 5 courses of masonry comprising exactly 100 stones, while the roof is spanned by 9 huge granite beams (all of them now cracked). Not only does its south wall lie exactly 365.24235 P" beyond the midpoint of the antechamber. With its breadth from north to south of 10 royal cubits, its length from east to west of 20 Royal Cubits and its height of 230.3871 P", the largest triangle that can be inserted into the chamber (comprising length, end-diagonal and cubic diagonal) has exactly the 'Pythagorean' ratio of 3:4:5.

This may seem surprising in view of the Pyramid's early date. Yet it is by no means all. Mathematicians will further appreciate the following even more extraordinary data:

Length: 2×365.24235 P" $\div \sqrt{\pi}$
Breadth: 365.24235 P" $\div \sqrt{\pi}$
Height: $\sqrt{(5 \times 365.24235 \text{ P}")} \div 2\sqrt{\pi}$
Floor diagonal: $\sqrt{(5 \times 365.24235 \text{ P}")} \div \sqrt{\pi}$
End-wall diagonal: 3×365.24235 P" $\div 2\sqrt{\pi}$
Side-wall diagonal: $\sqrt{(21 \times 365.24235 \text{ P}")} \div 2\sqrt{\pi}$
Cubic diagonal: 5×365.24235 P" $\div 2\sqrt{\pi}$

On top of this, the sum of the squares of all seven dimensions, measured in units of 5 royal cubits, totals exactly 100, while the sum of the three principal dimensions of the empty, lidless granite coffer that occupies the chamber's western end works out at exactly one-fifth of the sum of the three principal dimensions of the chamber itself.

And the interior of the coffer, as Petrie himself revealed, has been hollowed out of a solid block of granite with jewelled drills *under pressures of no less than two tonnes.*

The facts, clearly, are little less than staggering. Yet they are also highly significant.

The almost obsessive reference to π and the number 365.24235, plus the fact that the position apparently intended for the southern end of the coffer itself lies just 365.24235 P" beyond the entrance to the antechamber, strongly suggests that the chamber represents nothing less than spacetime itself. Moreover, the fact that the length of the coffer is equal to the width of the chamber minus 116.26 P" (which is, of course, equal to 365.24235 P" $\div \pi$) dramatically announces *some kind of breakout from time and space (compare circles in diagram on page 161)*.

The other features proceed to indicate the actual manner of this breakout. Of the two 'air shafts' that open to north and south some 80 P" to the right of the passage axis, and with their tops 41.21 P" above the floor, the northern, rectangular one clearly represents (in terms of the reconstructed code) a channel for physical influences to enter from 'outside'. But the southern one, with its extraordinary, womb-like entrance and its initially circular cross section, evidently represents a channel of non-terrestrial escape and rebirth.

Above the chamber, moreover, lie five further chambers of indeterminate shape and constructed in decreasing amounts of granite, culminating in a huge, upward-pointing *limestone* gable that apparently indicates a final ascent from Earth. Evidently, then, the chamber and its superincumbent multi-chamber complex represent *a multi-stage transition to some higher, albeit perfectly physical world that will involve the transcending of spacetime itself.*

'In my Father's house,' it might be said, 'are many mansions.'

Moreover, the lowest of the chambers is directly connected by a rough tunnel to the top section of the Grand Gallery. If original, it apparently suggests that there is some direct connection between the highest (albeit 'suspended') insights and imaginings attained by humanity hitherto and the new, multi-level dispensation into which it is about to enter – almost as if the one has succeeded in directly anticipating the other. The suggestion is no more than logical, and ties in intriguingly with early 20th-century developments in futuristic science and science fiction.

3989   2989

The King's Chamber initiative

The rough, painted hieroglyphs are probably 19th-century forgeries[20,37]

From 2989, terrestrial mortals will enter a thousand-year era of final transformation and emergence. In the course of it, time and space will be totally transcended and potential death transformed into actual survival, thanks to a multi-stage perfecting process that will have involved leaving Earth behind and journeying to another physical world elsewhere in the cosmos.

This announcement is necessarily dramatic, and curiously reminiscent of the kind of message that the so-called 'Religions of the Book' (Judaism, Christianity, Islam) have long been beaming at us. Yet it is very different, too. All of them have proclaimed the existence of a 'higher world' and promised eventual access to it for those humans willing to fulfil its demanding entry conditions. Christianity has even envisaged humanity going to meet the coming Messiah in the clouds. But none of them has suggested that this might envisage a physical journey into the cosmos, or that the promised new world under a new heaven might turn out to be quite literally that.

Still less have they indicated just where that world might lie.

This, however, is precisely what the Great Pyramid now proceeds to do. For the orientation of the all-important southern 'air shaft' is quite precise. Like a laser it pinpoints (for the established reference era, at least) one particular target in the sky. Bauval and his colleagues have long since determined what that target is.

It is the belt of Orion. And not merely the belt in general, but one star in particular.

That star is Al Nitak, or ζ Orionis.

This is a truly vital piece of information. It would clearly have been unwise to let its transmission depend purely on the survival of a single shaft and the indeterminate accuracy of some yet-to-be devised computer program. We should expect there to be the most definite and unmistakable of checks somewhere on site.

And indeed, there is. Just in case there should be any doubt about it, the designer built *the Great Pyramid itself*. For on the great Giza star map, as we have seen, the Pyramid takes up on the ground the relative position of Al Nitak in the sky.

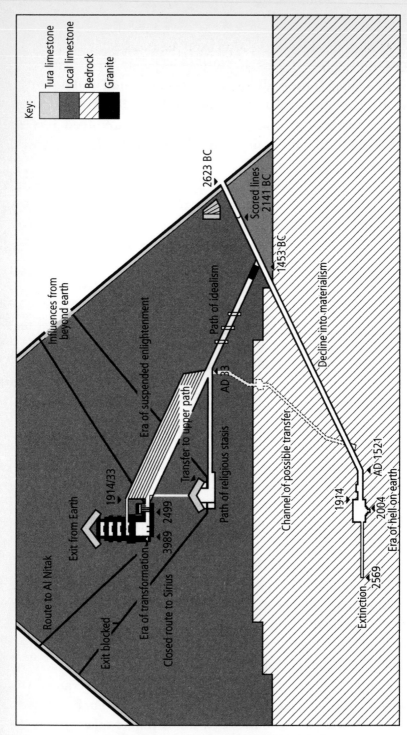

Key:

Tura limestone
Local limestone
Bedrock
Granite

Influences from beyond earth

Route to Al Nitak

Exit blocked

Exit from Earth

1914/33

Era of suspended enlightenment

Era of transformation

3989 2499

Closed route to Sirius

Transfer to upper path

Path of religious stasis

Path of idealism

AD 33

2623 BC

Scored lines
2141 BC

1453 BC

Decline into materialism

Channel of possible transfer

1914

AD 1521

2004

Era of hell on earth

Extinction

2569

Summary chart of the Great Pyramid initiative

178

Al Nitak, in short, is the Alpha and the Omega, the First and the Last, the origin and the goal.

That, then, is where our gaze must now turn.

STARWATCH
SIX

THE GODS ARE WAITING. Far away on a distant blue planet their emissaries have at last made contact, established friendly relations, revealed what must occur. The cycles of time have been explained, the destiny of the planet and its neighbours laid bare, the true nature and purpose of their life revealed.

The inhabitants on Earth have responded, some with incredulity, some with credulity – and a few with true understanding.

It is with these that the emissaries have duly embarked on an intense and demanding programme of education. In the course of it their pupils have learnt to understand the world on which they live. They have learnt to understand space and time, and the laws that govern both.

And they have learnt to understand themselves.

Little by little they have been taught the science and technology that must underlie the next stage in their evolution. They have been given the tools and shown how to use them. They have been shown the priorities that must govern the culminating stage in the Great Initiative.

And now they are ready.

Embarking in their great starships, they set out on their long Odyssey. As Earth recedes into nothingness and only imponderables and unknowns seem to lie ahead, even the strongest hearts tremble. Is this really the right path? Can they trust what they have been told? Can they believe the unbelievable?

Fortunately, there is reassurance. Alongside them speed the Elohim themselves, resolutely headed in the same direction. Not for the first time, they are intimately presiding over an epoch-making exodus. They are the very Lords of Departure, the Masters of Movement, the Midwives of Worlds.

Like some mighty, cosmic hand, the spacedrive hurls them all forwards. The entire universe seems to spin and whirl. The very powers of heaven are shaken. Stars become streaks, then coalesce into a single, glowing spacebow.

The die is cast.

What will the future hold?

17

THE
KINGDOM
OF
ORION

ORION IS NOT ONLY the most brilliant of the constellations. It is also one of the prime stellar nurseries of our galaxy. Situated along one of the latter's spiral arms, it is a region where stars are even now being born.

Originally the constellation was nothing more than a huge, diffuse cloud of gas. As little as 12 million years ago (by current estimates) this gradually started to condense, first into dust, and then into bright young stars. In time, this process of condensation spread from the region in the top right of the star map overleaf towards the galactic south. By about 8 million years ago it had reached the region of Orion's Belt. Some of the young stars in the Sword appear to have condensed out as little as 2 million years ago.

The whole of Orion's development, in other words, has taken place very much since the disappearance of Earth's dinosaurs. Had the 'terrible lizards' ever looked up at the night sky, they would have seen little more than a large 'hole in the sky' where the great gas cloud was blotting out the myriad stars beyond.

Within the cloud, and protected by its darkness, meanwhile, a whole range of complex molecules were gradually developing –

especially as the rising pressures generated by the condensation process produced correspondingly higher temperatures. Astronomers have already identified over 30 different ones (including all the hydrogen-, nitrogen- and carbon-based compounds that are known to be the basic building blocks of life) in the dark region behind the Great Orion Nebula alone (*see star map opposite*) – and this necessarily only in its *outer* regions. What lies within is unknown. The other dark areas that survive necessarily contain similar molecular riches.

As young stars started to form, however, areas of the original cloud started to be 'lit up' by their radiation. Since this radiation naturally included ultraviolet light, it had the effect of eventually stripping all the molecules of their atoms again, leaving in these areas only diffuse clouds composed mainly of hydrogen.

In the Great Nebula (*see 'The Sword' opposite*) this process can still be seen in action. For some 15 light years in each direction (equivalent to the perceived diameter of the moon), the whole area of surviving gas and dust glows with the brilliant light of over 100 young stars (nearly half of them already with distinct protoplanetary discs), plus innumerable others that are in the very process of being born. In particular, it glows not only with the red light of irradiated hydrogen, but also with the green light emitted by oxygen atoms and the bluish and ultraviolet radiations of molecules in the dust cloud, which also emit powerful radio waves.

This light does not come free, of course. All of these latter atoms and molecules are being steadily 'cooked'. The light emanating from them is the pale light of death. The time will come when only the soft glow of hydrogen remains. Within the so-called 'Trapezium' at the core of the Nebula, a new star cluster as bright as 100,000 suns is even now being formed. In this region, then, Death is already fully enthroned.

But if Death is steadily advancing through the Nebula, when did the process begin? On the available evidence, not much more than 12 million years ago. Before that, there were long aeons of time when the original Orionic cloud remained dark, diffuse and rich with forming chemicals. So dark and so diffuse was it that, to any

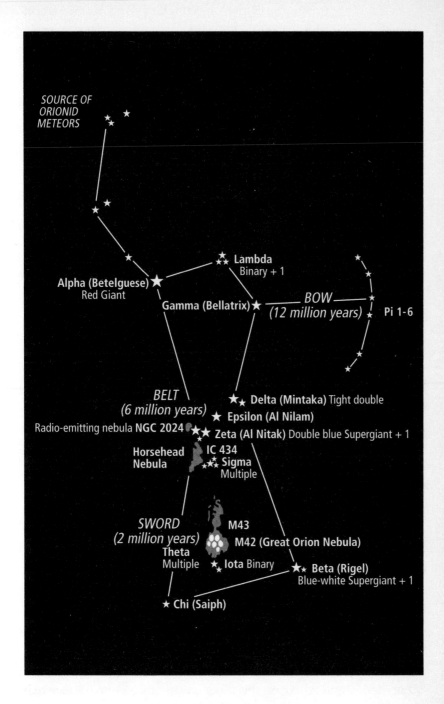

SOURCE OF ORIONID METEORS

Alpha (Betelguese)
Red Giant

Gamma (Bellatrix)

Lambda
Binary + 1

BOW
(12 million years)

Pi 1-6

BELT
(6 million years)

Radio-emitting nebula **NGC 2024**

Horsehead Nebula

IC 434

Delta (Mintaka) Tight double

Epsilon (Al Nilam)

Zeta (Al Nitak) Double blue Supergiant + 1

Sigma
Multiple

SWORD
(2 million years)
Theta
Multiple

M43

M42 (Great Orion Nebula)

Iota Binary

Beta (Rigel)
Blue-white Supergiant + 1

Chi (Saiph)

Schematic details of Orion

185

watching dinosaur, it must have blotted out even more of the night sky than Orion currently illumines.

What, then, was happening within the cloud? Here we can at present only speculate. Yet some are better qualified to speculate than others.

In his well-known novel *The Black Cloud* of 1957[15], the eminent Cambridge astronomer Fred Hoyle (now *Sir* Fred) advanced the possibility that interstellar clouds might actually be more promising breeding grounds for life than the restricting gravity fields of planets such as Earth. Wisely arguing through the mouths of his protagonists rather than directly, he theorized that, once temperatures were favourable – thanks to received starlight, or perhaps encouraged in the present case by the early stages of star condensation – molecules of varying complexity might be laid down on the surfaces of larger particles within the cloud. These molecules in turn might then start to react electrically with each other. As silicon chips have amply demonstrated since Hoyle wrote his book, such electrical discharges need not be very large to provide the working mechanism for what would, in effect, be a kind of living, evolving, self-designed computer. The apparent haphazardness of the process would, of course, be no greater than is generally supposed to have characterized the corresponding process on Earth, and would be amply compensated for by the almost unlimited – indeed, literally unimaginable – amount of time available, which would be far greater than that available for the terrestrial equivalent. Later, larger voltages might be used to generate magnetic fields that could permit the cloud gently to reshuffle its contents for optimal electrical effect.

In this way the entire dark cloud might, after a time, become a single, living brain. None of its energies would need to be wasted on resisting gravity, or on moving from place to place, or even on looking for food. Its food would be there, all around it, in the form of radiated starlight from nearby suns. Even if it were temporarily to run out, it could happily feed on its own substance by allowing parts of itself to condense into stars.

For 'dark cloud', then, on this model, read 'intelligence'. But what an intelligence! Even the surviving clouds in the Great Nebula are each some 150 light years long, and contain enough matter to make over 100,000 stars. In the case of the original Orionic cloud itself, these figures can be multiplied many times over. Assuming that it organized itself into a single intelligence, then, rather than into a series of discrete mini-intelligences (as the very nature of electrical communications within the cloud would tend to ensure), it would be a brain the size of a mini-universe. Unrestricted by any pre-set biological structure, it could not only think thoughts that are far beyond anything that we could ever imagine, but put them (as far as it was concerned) into instantaneous effect.

Except, of course, that for any thought to travel at the speed of light all the way through the cloud would take hundreds, if not thousands of years. This might argue for a degree of area special-ization. But then, on the other hand, what is a mere thousand years to an intelligence of this order?

Nevertheless, life is never without its problems. In the case of the Orionic cloud, the main one would concern star formation. The tendency of any cloud in space is slowly to condense under the pull of its own admittedly extremely diffuse gravity. 100,000 stars ultimately weigh quite a lot, after all. Unless, therefore, the cloud were able to develop the means (possibly magnetic) of con-trolling this process, successive parts of itself would gradually con-dense, heat up and turn into young, hot stars. It would, in effect, undergo a whole series of little deaths, or a kind of spreading can-cer. With a cloud as large as the original Orionic one, this process could go on for millions of years without seriously diminishing the intelligence's ability to think its thoughts or be itself. Eventually, though, it would start to prove life-threatening.

On the other hand, the very same process would provide more electrical 'food' for the rest of the cloud to think its thoughts and develop its capabilities. Possibly this increased supply, supplement-ing that derived from the radiation of nearby suns, would actually be regarded as useful by the cloud. Perhaps, then, it would actively encourage the process. Moreover, if it did, it could presumably choose just where to provoke the various star condensations into occurring.

If, in other words, it wished to arrange the stars of Orion's Belt in a straight line, it would not even need to push them around as we surmised earlier: *instead, it could simply choose where to condense them out in the first place.*

Yet ultimately the process must run up against its own limitations. The cloud's substance, after all, is not infinite. What, then, can be done? Only one avenue of salvation seems to offer itself: the intelligence must in some way 'mind-meld' with some other intelligence that exists *on the other side* of the black hole of its own extinction – *an intelligence that has somehow managed to develop on one of the cooling planetary bodies that have condensed out of the discs of gas and dust surrounding the deadly newborn stars.*

Or rather, it must seek – or even seed – some much older planet so as to give such an intelligence time to develop. For it has to be said that any planets that exist across the vast expanses of Orion – whether around the stars of the Belt or anywhere else – are likely to be far too young as yet to support life. Many of them, indeed, are probably still molten.

That distant planetary intelligence would, of course, have to be extremely advanced. It would have to be sympathetic to the greater, Orionic intelligence. And, above all, it would have to consent. None of these is a foregone conclusion. The last of them might be all the more likely, though, if life on the planet in question were known to be threatened with imminent extinction.

But how might contact be made and consent be obtained? Electronic surveillance and eventual communication might well be possible – though this narrow, channelled form of contact would of course be no substitute for the direct, broad spectrum contact on which the ultimate merging process would ultimately depend. Ultimately some kind of actual visit would be necessary – either by the bearers of the new intelligence to the cloud, or by the cloud to the new, planetary intelligence.

But the latter might lack the technology, to say nothing of the will and trust – and the cloud itself, of course, would be constitutionally incapable of making the trip. Even with the aid of gravity control, there would be tremendous problems of inertia. Besides, shifting a mass equivalent to 100,000 suns would disrupt the whole of local space. Instead, though, it could perhaps concentrate small parts of itself into localized vortices with the aid of strong magnetic fields and shoot these off as probes into the void.

So that what eventually arrived on the surface of the chosen planet would be a very strange spectacle indeed – a kind of whirling vortex of dust and 'smoke', carrying a high electrical charge and emitting all kinds of strange acoustic and optical effects.

This, it will be recalled, is precisely what the biblical Israelites seem to have encountered on Mount Horeb over 3000 years ago.

The mountain, it is claimed, was covered by a thick cloud from which issued thunderings and lightnings. It was death for anybody to draw near. Even when the sacred tabernacle was constructed – well away from the camp – as a travelling venue for meeting the 'Elohim', it was still enveloped in a 'pillar of cloud' that, at night, was 'full of fire'. The same 'pillar of cloud' subsequently guarded the tribes' onward march. And indeed, the Divine presence would be thought of in this way for ever after.

Perhaps it is relevant, then, that the contemporary Mycenean Greeks likewise associated the lordly entity that they in turn called 'Zeus' or 'sky father' directly with thunderclouds and lightning bolts.

Could there, then – to coin a phrase – be some fire beneath this whole column of speculative and mythological smoke? In view of the likely lack of habitable planets in Orion, are the Elohim in reality not planetary beings at all, but vast interstellar presences much older than ourselves? Might they even be the ultimate fathers of life on this planet – and on countless other worlds as well? Could it be, indeed, that there are in reality not many Elohim, but only one (the Hebrew word, curiously, is a plural that is treated as a singular), with each emanation being merely a cloned part of itself – much as the 'Religions of the Book' have always claimed?

And could it be that its own ultimate survival is as much at stake as ours?

18

THE
HALLS
OF
VISHNU

AT ABOUT THE SAME TIME as the Israelites were experiencing their traumatic encounter at Sinai, something not unrelated seems also to have been happening far to the east. The Indian *Vedas*, or ritual hymns, were in the process of being formulated. Their subsequent texts still survive today. In the course of them the great god Vishnu – co-member, with Brahma the Creator and Shiva the Destroyer, of the supreme trinity of gods – gradually takes form. Usually he is represented in art as youthful *and blue*. His primary act in the *Rig Veda*[34] is to take *three mighty steps* into the cosmos, there to establish the 'upper dwelling place' where, *with his consort Lakshmi*, he now resides:

> Could I but reach his refuge place so dear
> Where those rejoice who all the gods adore,
> Close to far-striding Vishnu drawing near,
> His highest step, life's sweet fount evermore! (I.154)

From there he chooses from time to time to intervene in human affairs. 'Whenever, order, justice and morality are in peril,' runs a

later text, 'I descend to earth and take human form.' Of the resulting *avatars*, the future *Kalki* is (as we noted earlier) the tenth and
final one. *A giant with a horse's head,* he will bring to a close the 'Age
of Iron' (i.e. the present age) and destroy the wicked. The instrument of this dramatic initiative will be *a fiery sword like a comet.* The
universe will then be re-absorbed into the Absolute until the next
cycle of creation.

What is stunning about this whole tradition is not primarily its
imagery, however. *It is the fact that it paints an accurate picture of the
star Al Nitak and the neighbouring regions of Orion.*

The three stars of Orion's belt; the blue giant itself and its celestial
companion; the horse's head; the sword which, as in reality, has the
fiery nebulosity of a comet's tail – all is faithfully described. Yet the
Horsehead Nebula in particular is invisible to the naked eye. So, for
that matter, is the blueness of Al Nitak. Failing the use of some kind
of telescope, therefore, this whole tradition suggests an early source
that had seen these phenomena from much closer.

Who else, then, but the Elohim?

Yet, as we have seen, it is unlikely that they – or it – currently
inhabit any planet in the Belt of Orion, still less around Al Nitak
itself. The thick clouds of the Horsehead Nebula may be more
promising, but are possibly too cold (the darker shading in the
cloud-map above represents hotter clouds *behind* the Horsehead,
illuminated by the source IC 434). The Great Orion Nebula, on the
other hand, with its newly forming stars, is by now far too hot for
life, though the dark cloud behind it is a possibility. The fact that
the small nebula NGC 2024, just to the left of Al Nitak, is a powerful radio emitter suggests that it, too, is already becoming quite hot
on the side facing Al Nitak (*compare colour plates*), but deeper within the cloud or on its far side conditions for life may be much more
propitious.

Yet it is seemingly towards Al Nitak that the southern shaft of
the Great Pyramid's King's Chamber uncompromisingly points –
while the Pyramid itself massively verifies the fact on the ground.
The planned destination must therefore lie very close to the great
blue, double supergiant.

But where?

Once again, the solid facts on the ground ought to provide the ultimate clue. Yet what clues are there at Giza, if any? Surely the Elohim would not have omitted to add this final piece to the puzzle?

The current map of Giza, as Bauval and his colleagues have shown, is orientated to fit the celestial situation at 10,500 BC. Our first task, therefore, has to be to re-orientate it to fit the current stellar layout. This gives the ground plan on page 194 (overleaf).

Somewhere on this plan, then, the vital clue should lie. And the first point to notice is that there is absolutely no indication of anything significant anywhere to the north of the pyramids (bottom of picture) – or thus to the celestial south of Orion's Belt. At once, therefore, both the dark cloud behind the Great Orion Nebula and the similarly dark Horse's Head are ruled out (*compare colour plates*). As we search the area to the left of the Great Pyramid, however, we do come across something.

Namely the so-called Trial Passages.

Generally closed off to the public, and often deliberately filled with rubble from other excavations, these important excavations in the rock some 100 metres to the east of the Great Pyramid are often written off by visitors as some kind of 'tomb' (*see diagram page 55*), despite the fact that no other tomb even remotely resembles them. Even most authors of books on the pyramids, consequently, are unaware of their existence. Yet, as we saw earlier, they contain prototypes of all the Great Pyramid's main passageways except the King's Chamber passage to their correct lateral dimensions. If, then, as seems certain, they were excavated *before* the Pyramid was constructed, they cannot help but be original.

Indeed, they have to be more than that. They are the very 'seed' or 'source' of the plan that was subsequently to be laid out in three-dimensional solid stone within the Great Pyramid itself.

But this, surely, is precisely what we are looking for. On the cosmic scale, too, what we are seeking is the *source* – that same source that, for us, turns out to be also our future goal.

But there is a further mystery. Immediately to the south of the Trial Passages (i.e. above them on the map) a large pit opens in the

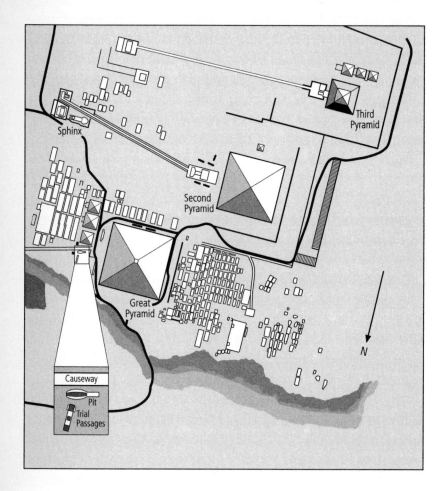

The original Giza ground plan, as re-oriented to the stars

rock. Ostensibly designed to hold a pharaonic 'sky boat', it lies hard alongside the ritual causeway that formerly ran from the Great Pyramid down to the Nile Delta. The clear impression comes across that Trial Passages, boat pit and causeway are in some way intimately connected.

The impression is strengthened when it is realized that the boat-pit is quite unlike any other. The four other pits alongside the Pyramid's base are either rectangular or vaguely boat-shaped. This one, too, is more or less boat-shaped in its deeper part, but towards the surface it becomes more bottle-shaped, or even fish-shaped (see blow-up diagram above).

And that fish is swimming not *up* the causeway towards the Pyramid, but determinedly *down* it towards the fertile flatlands of the Delta.

Or perhaps it is not a fish. The bottom of the pit, certainly, says 'sky boat'. But its upper part says 'receptacle' or 'container' – and its proximity to the causeway says *mobile* receptacle or container' into the bargain. Could it, then, be a representation of a *starship*?

The suggestion may seem fantastic. It could have been dreamt up by Erich von Däniken. Yet from 'sky boat' to 'starship' is not such an enormous step, if indeed it is a step at all. What if the an-cient gods chose to show through this particular pit that they are indeed one and the same?

The upshot would be stunning. For it would be that we have before us *an actual route map to the stars*. The pit signifies the future space ark or arks, the Trial Passages the whole plan's place of origin – *and the causeway the final route from Al Nitak towards the ultimate en-counter with the Elohim.*

But why, in that case, were the Trial Passages sited *here*, at this particular point on the map? Clearly they could have been exca-vated anywhere on the Giza plateau. Yet it was *this* spot that was chosen. Presumably, then, it was chosen for a reason. The obvious question therefore poses itself.

What corresponds in the sky to the Trial Passages on the ground?

Comparison of Earth map and star map immediately yields the answer. *The corresponding feature is the bright luminosity that is labelled*

'NGC 2024' (colour plates), and that figures so prominently in the map on page 185. This area of cloud, constantly feeding on the radiated heat of the neighbouring star Al Nitak, and connected as it is to the rest of the general Orion B Cloud, may indeed represent one of the few warm, chemically-rich regions still left that are capable of supporting the Orionic intelligence. *Moreover, the shape and orientation of the Trial Passages seem specifically to reflect the dark, oblique gas lane that can be seen crossing in front of NGC 2024 in the photograph (colour plates).*

There can really be little doubt about it. The rendezvous with the Elohim – if rendezvous it is meant to be – is destined to take place *in the vicinity of that glowing cloud.* Not, perhaps, on the hot side of it immediately exposed to Al Nitak, but certainly (as the directional logic of the Trial Passages suggests) at some cooler point beyond the northern end of the gas lane. It may yet be, in short, that we are indeed destined (just as the scriptures curiously suggest) to go to meet our future saviour *in the clouds.*

The Great Pyramid's causeway confirms these details – for it leads not directly *to* the Trial Passages, but *around the back of them* (*compare diagram page 194*). Like the boat pit itself, in other words, the great encounter must (if we are reading the directions aright) take place while the space arks are parked in space just to the galactic north of the cloud.

This means, of course, that there is no possibility of our staying there. There are almost certainly no planets near the cloud – and, unlike the Elohim, we are not interstellar intelligences. That, in fact, is the whole point of the exercise. What has to ensue is presumably a prolonged and intense interchange of information leading to an actual merging of consciousness. *But then the journey must continue.*

This is precisely what the Great Pyramid seems to indicate in its King's Chamber complex. Above the culminating King's Chamber, whose granite apparently symbolizes the great mid-space Orion encounter, lie five more ill-defined chambers composed of ever-decreasing amounts of granite and ever-growing amounts of limestone. Evidently there are five more worlds to visit, each more and more earthlike, until in the topmost chamber of all the future travellers, having completed their programme of intensive evolution, reach a world like home.

A new Earth, under a new heaven.

Which no doubt is why the causeway itself seems to proclaim the selfsame message. After the encounter with the Trial Passages its route, too, lies onward. And eventually, after vaulting into space off the edge of the plateau, it comes down to the green and fertile Delta, suggesting humanity's final descent on to a world comparable to Egypt itself – but an Egypt still young and golden, burgeoning amid Earth's ancient springtime.

Unless it lies in a different galaxy entirely, then, that world will probably lie a good deal closer to the galactic centre than Al Nitak. It will be an older world than the planets currently forming all across Orion. But in Earth terms it will be a new world entirely, unspoilt by pollution or over-exploitation – a new, virgin planet on which humanity and Elohim alike can forge a new, advanced civilization that may yet become a beacon to the rest of the galaxy.

All clearly depends, then, on confirming the initial destination. That will no doubt be one of the tasks of the four preliminary encounters indicated by the Great Pyramid's antechamber. But if it is indeed Al Nitak and the nearby luminous nebulosity IC 2024, then we have a problem on our hands.

Normally classed as a binary, Al Nitak is in fact a triple star some 19,000 times brighter that our own sun. It consists of two enormous suns (of second and fourth magnitude respectively) slowly orbiting each other in tight embrace, together with a more distant tenth-magnitude companion.

Stunningly, even these facts seem to have been memorialized at Giza.

For, as we noted in Chapter 19, the original pyramids produced noticeable optical effects. That seems to have been one of the reasons why the surface of the Great Pyramid in particular was honed and polished to such an astonishing degree of accuracy. 'Optical', indeed, was precisely the word used of it by Petrie. The result was a set of reflections which, at noon of the summer solstice, produced *the unmistakable shape of a star* (the phenomenon, as we have noted, is not difficult to demonstrate with the aid of a polished scale model). True, observing it would have been a problem, but it might have become apparent in conditions of thick haze, and could certainly have been mapped out on the ground with the aid of an army of observers equipped with stakes.

But the surface of Second Pyramid, too, was polished: indeed the remains of that superb finish can still be observed today. The summit of the great monument still gleams in the moonlight, or glows like a snow-capped mountain peak in the early morning sun.

As for the Third Pyramid, its lower courses were (as we have seen) originally clad in red granite, which was left undressed – conceivably in order to *avoid* such optical effects. Its upper courses, however, were very probably finished in the same dressed, white limestone as the other two. In this way its designers contrived to combine *three separate* symbolisms – through its height and its red granite casing that of Mars, through its geographical position that of the star Mintaka in Orion's belt, and though the reflections of its much-reduced white upper portion, that of a considerably smaller star.

At noon of the summer solstice, then, *all three* reflections might have been observed – *and their respective proportions would have closely mirrored those of the three component suns of Al Nitak itself (see diagram opposite).*

Whether the three satellite pyramids to the east of the Great Pyramid – or the further four attending the Second and Third – represent planets orbiting the corresponding stars of Zeta Orionis, meanwhile, is a question which our technology is not yet sufficiently advanced to determine...

The ancient gods, then, seem to have been well aware of the true nature of Al Nitak and its immediate environment. But if they were aware of its triune nature, they must also have been aware of its enormous size. Perhaps that, too, is what is deliberately reflected in the pyramids' huge bulk.

But to the potential travellers of AD 2499 the problem will not be such enormity. It will be sheer distance.

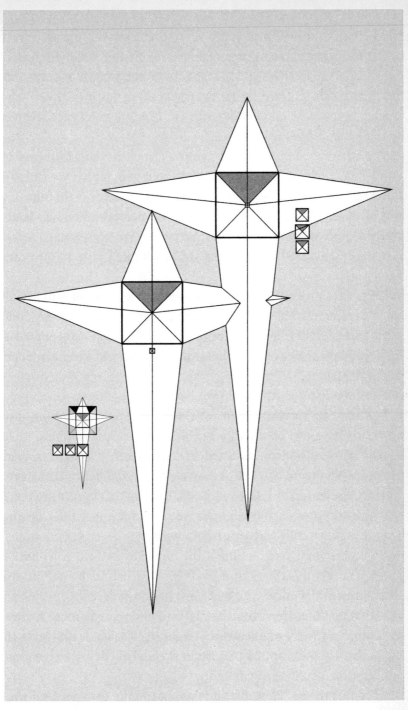

Star-shaped noon reflections of the main Giza pyramids at midsummer
with contrast exaggerated

Al Nitak, after all, lies some 1,100 light years from us (even though some earlier sources suggest as much as 1,500 light years). So, clearly, does NGC 2024. Light, in other words, takes 1,100 years to reach us from them, even travelling (as it is always observed to do) at 300,000 kilometres (or 186,000 miles) per second.

Or rather, it used to.

The very speed of light itself, after all, means that astronomy is at least as much about history as it is about geography. We can say nothing about even our own sun that is not already eight minutes out of date. Whatever we say about the nearest star to us is already $4\frac{1}{2}$ years behind the times. Whatever we say about Al Nitak is actually ancient history, since we last looked at it 1,100 years ago.

Any astronomer who uses the present tense about distant galaxies is thus inevitably talking through his or her hat. If every full-sized galaxy in the universe beyond our own had disappeared a million years since, no astronomical paper would yet have even noted the fact.

For nobody on Earth would yet have seen it.

We need to be wary, then, of this effect. Calculating the distances of stars can be a tricky business at the best of times. That is why those distances, as listed in the reference books, vary so much. Al Nitak and NGC 2024 may well lie 1,100 light years away. At least, they used to 1,100 years ago. But time and space are eternally functions of each other, and we shall not know the true answer until we finally break out from both.

No doubt, then, the Elohim of the antechamber era will give us more accurate information *in good time* – which is, by definition, where any initial encounter will have to *take place*.

Let us assume, however, that 1,100 light years is more or less the true distance. This means that light itself takes 1,100 years to make the trip. And nothing, Einstein is widely believed to have established, can go faster than light.

Does this mean, then, that it is going to take us over a millennium to get there? Can we survive that long *en route*? Would we even want to?

Fortunately, the cherished belief owes more to medieval mind-sets among modern scientists than it does to scientific fact.

Let alone Einstein.

But perhaps we should let Einstein speak for himself...

19

NOTHING
CAN
GO
FASTER
THAN
EINSTEIN

EINSTEIN'S WHOLE THEORY OF RELATIVITY[5, 9] is based on one simple premise. *Light*, it accepts, *can only travel at the speed of light*.

This, it has to be admitted, is pretty logical.

Given, however, that light is all that we have to observe the rest of the universe with, the fact has some extremely far-reaching implications for how things seem to us. On the other hand, it is much less likely to tell us much about how things actually are. Still less is it likely to tell us anything new about that observed limitation itself.

It needs to be established at the outset, then, what any theory of relativity is by definition about – and consequently, too, what it is by definition *not* about. A theory of relativity (in the Einsteinian sense, at least) is a theory about how the observer relates to the observed, and about how the observed relates to the observer. It is not – nor was Einstein's ever intended to be – a theory about either the observer or the observed *in themselves*. If it deals (as Einstein's does) with velocity, mass and energy, then it is with velocity, mass and energy not as absolutes, but *as they appear to the observer*. Exactly the same goes for time.

Einstein himself liked to exemplify this in very down-to-earth terms that would nowadays be considered politically somewhat incorrect. Five minutes sitting on a hot stove, he explained, can seem a very long time indeed. Five minutes sitting with a pretty girl, by contrast, does not seem nearly long enough.

In the Theory of Relativity, then, we can expect to find statements about *relationships*: we should not expect to find statements about *absolutes*.

A. THE FUNDAMENTAL POSTULATES

1. The Non-existence of the Ether

As a result of Thomas Young's famous double-slit experiment of 1803,[18] Einstein had long known that light, as it spreads from a light source such as the sun, behaves *like waves*. The fact that it also behaves *like particles* (as Einstein himself demonstrated in 1905) did not alter the fact in any way – though it did raise the worrying possibility of the existence of a kind of particulate mongrel that begged to be dubbed a *wavicle*.

Now if there were *waves* (at least, so it had been argued), then something had to be *waving*. That 'something' was presumably some kind of static, diffuse, luciferous medium pervading the entire universe, rather like water in a pond.

It was duly dubbed *the ether*.

A celebrated series of experiments was performed during the last two decades of the 19th century to detect this supposed ether. Again and again their results agreed. Their unanimity, in fact, was quite resounding. *The more they looked for the ether, the more it wasn't there.*

This led to Einstein's first basic postulate: *The ether does not exist.*

Now this conclusion was worrying. If there was no still ether for light to propagate itself through, then there was no still *anything*. The universe was not floating in some kind of etheric pond after all. There was no shore, no rocky island, no bottom, nor anything else for it to anchor itself to. It was drifting who knows how fast relative to who knows what. If it was afloat in anything, it was a sea of uncertainty.

Since this seems contrary to common sense, some later theorists have surmised that 'stillness' *does* exist, but only *relative to local gravitational fields*.

All motion, then, was relative. Neither motion nor speed could be absolute. Which was why all the basic formulae of Einstein's theory would in due course contain the quantity *v*, which stands not for 'real' velocity, but for *observed velocity relative to the observer*.

But then what else would you expect to hear from a theory of relativity?

'Excuse me,' an apocryphal Einstein once asked an equally apocryphal porter, 'does Crewe stop at this train?'

2. The Constant Relative Velocity of Light

Other 19th century experiments, meanwhile, had established that light – or at least, all the light that we can detect – always travels at a constant speed of 300,000 kilometres per second (or 186,000 miles per second). At all events, that was what all the various experiments measured it as doing. *But relative to what?* Since it could no longer be relative to the non-existent ether, logic suggested that it must be relative to the light source.

But logic proved to be wrong.

Subsequent astronomical experiments suggested quite unequivocally that the speed of light was *constant relative to the observer*. No matter how fast you travelled, or in which direction, in other words, light always arrived at your eyes *at the speed of light*.

This, of course, was baffling – if in another way rather obvious. Many people refused to believe it. Others tried to explain it, or to insist that the experiments were wrong. Only one man – Einstein – was big enough to do the obvious.

He simply accepted it.

The result was his second basic postulate: *the velocity of light is always constant relative to an observer.* In his equations this constant velocity of light would be represented by the letter c.

There may or may not be other light travelling at other speeds in the universe, in other words, but if so we cannot detect it. *Our* light always travels at c relative to ourselves.

B. THE SPECIAL THEORY

Einstein's ensuing Theory of Relativity is the result of a long series of rigorous mathematical calculations based on the two fundamental postulates. Those calculations are of course for advanced specialists, and will not be reproduced here. Their conclusions, however, are fairly easily explained – and, in the aggregate, remarkably commonsensical.

The Theory originally came in two parts. The first, which Einstein published in 1905, concerned only the implications for a body moving *at a constant velocity relative to the observer.* Cases involving acceleration of any kind were left for the all-inclusive General Theory, which did not appear until 11 years later. It is therefore the deductions of the Special Theory that I shall present here first.

1. The First Deduction: Contraction of Length

The first deduction states that, if two observers are moving at a constant speed relative to each other (whether towards each other, past each other or away from each other makes no difference), *everything about the other will appear to have shrunk in the direction of motion.* The effect is of course unnoticeable at the low speeds with which we are normally accustomed. But as those speeds approach the observed relative velocity of light itself, the effect becomes more and more pronounced until, as that velocity is reached, the observed length shrinks to zero and the traveller…simply disappears.

Not a word, note, about what has *actually* happened. Simply a lot of words about what *seems* to have happened. To the now-vanished traveller everything seems perfectly normal – *except that, to him or her, it is the original observer who will have disappeared.*

This is not quite as arch as it perhaps seems. Thanks to the very nature of our sensory systems, we do not observe things or people 'out there', but only *our observations* of things or people 'out there'. We 'see' not the objects themselves, but only the light that enters our eyes from their direction. As observers, in fact, we can never progress any further forward than the backs of our own eyeballs.

All that Einstein's first deduction does is to recognize the fact.

It also implies, incidentally, that nothing can be observed to travel faster than light relative to ourselves – for the simple reason that it will disappear first.

Which, given that light is what we are using to observe it with, seems pretty logical.

But then Einstein's fourth deduction (*see page 209*) deals with this point specifically.

2. The Second Deduction: Mass Increase with Velocity

The second deduction turns out, in the upshot, to be just as logical. It states that, when an object moves at a constant velocity in relation to yourself, its mass appears to increase in proportion to its observed relative speed towards, past or away from you. Once again, the effect is unobservable in everyday life. But at near-light speeds it seemingly becomes very pronounced, until at an observed relative velocity equal to that of light (and not, note, 'the speed of light', which is an impossible concept, for the simple reason that there is nothing static for that speed to be measured against), the object's mass becomes literally infinite.

If that object, meanwhile, happens to be another observer *observing you*, then (to him or her at least) *you* will have undergone the same transmogrification. Not only will you have busted all the (equally heavy) scales in the (equally heavy) supermarket on the (equally heavy) Earth. You will literally weigh as much as the (equally heavy) universe itself.

Which last may be an appalling prospect for inveterate slimmers, but is, in a strange, twisted way, oddly logical.

But then the whole thing is also logical in another way as well. For it means, in effect, that, even if, with the aid of some kind of remote energy beam, you were able to push your shopping trolley away so fast into the distance that it actually disappeared, you would be no more able to make it seem to go faster than light than if it were the heaviest thing in the universe. You would, in short, need all the energy that the universe contains and more.

Which – given that light is the only thing that can possibly mediate that 'seeming' – is once again no more than common sense.

3. The Third Deduction: Addition of Velocities

The third deduction states that the relative velocity of two steadily approaching observers (in separate space ships, say) always seems to each of them to be *less than* the sum of their velocities relative to some fixed point between them. Now of course there is *no* fixed point between them. But if you, as a kind of 'umpire' in this cosmic jousting match, chose to take a position somewhere in the middle, you would theoretically be perfectly able (perhaps by using a pair of double-angled mirrors) to see both ships approaching from either side at, say, just over half the observed relative speed of light – which means, of course, that they would be approaching each other at a relative speed equal to *more than* the observed relative speed of light (so once again scotching the popular idea that 'going faster than light' is impossible). Yet, *to each of the travellers themselves*, the other would seem to be approaching at *considerably less* than the observed relative speed of light.

The result, of course, could be spectacular. If both travellers failed, in consequence of their relativistically faulty instrument readings, to take evasive action in time, a nasty accident could result. For the instruments, even though they agreed with the theory, would certainly be *wrong*. But then you, too – for all your claimed status as a dispassionate observer – might be well advised to get out of the way well before the collision.

All of which amounts to saying that things can only seem to be doing what they seem to be doing.

Which is once again no more than logical.

4. The Fourth Deduction: The Maximum Observable Velocity

The fourth deduction is the most famous of all. It states that nothing can appear to the observer to travel faster than light relative to himself or herself. As we have seen, this, too, is perfectly logical, since light itself (or some other part of the familiar electromagnetic spectrum) is bound to be the medium for that appearing. But it is self-evidently a statement of appearance, not reality. If the observed object *were* travelling faster than the speed of light relative to the observer, he or she would – as the deduction requires – simply not see it.

Yet there is absolutely no obvious reason why it should not be doing so.

If the observer, for example, happened to be a member of the crew of a space ship travelling at the speed of light, its speed *relative to himself* would inevitably be zero. However fast it travelled, this would continue to be the case. Thus, even if the ship were to travel at five times the speed of light, the fourth deduction would be in no way violated.

True, some odd things would seem to be happening *outside* the ship. In particular, the stars immediately ahead and astern would (in line with the First Deduction) have disappeared completely, while the known constellations on either side would have grouped themselves closer and closer together until they formed a brilliant, but ever-narrowing ring abeam of the ship (this does not of course mean, however, that even a single star would *actually* have moved). They would also (in accordance with the Second and Third Deductions) have thinned into what appeared to be flat discs rather than spheres, as well as apparently becoming extra-ordinarily heavy.

Navigation, in consequence, would be posing some interesting problems.

Inside the ship, however, everything would appear to be perfectly normal. The rest of the crew would neither be flattening out into mere two-dimensional cardboard cutouts, nor flattening any chairs that they happened to sit on.

So that the 'speed of light' (which is in any case a pure fiction since, as we noted earlier, there is absolutely nothing static for it to be measured against) is not the insuperable barrier that otherwise intelligent scientists often suppose it to be – or not, at least, for any reason stated in Einstein's Theory.

This tendency to erect imagined barriers to future progress in the field of travel is a strange, but well-established one. To medieval sailors, the imagined barrier was the edge of the world. Even Columbus's crew were allegedly worried about this one, despite the fact that Columbus knew perfectly well that the Earth was round before he set off, and apparently had maps to prove it.[13]

By Victorian times, the ground had shifted somewhat. With the advent of the railways in the 1840s, the conviction became widespread that any steam train travelling at more than 30 miles per hour would automatically cause its passengers to suffocate. True, many of them nearly did – especially in the tunnels – but it was assuredly not because of their speed.

The next imagined barrier was the speed of sound. Indeed, with the development of the jet aircraft the idea of 'the sound barrier' became an established concept. The term was even made the title of a book – and a film. True, compressibility problems did make it necessary to redesign airframes somewhat. But eventually test pilots succeeded during the late 1940s and early 1950s in showing that the imagined barrier was no more insuperable than any other. Indeed, even passenger aircraft such as Concorde nowadays have not the slightest problem in flying at *twice* the speed of sound.

And so modern scientific theorists have shifted their ground even further. The goal posts have been moved yet again. Nowadays the ultimate barrier is supposed to be the speed of light (even though, as we have seen, it does not actually have a 'speed' at all). To an extraordinary extent the modern experts resemble medieval theologians issuing dire warnings about the dangers of approaching the edge of God's world and falling into Hell. In both cases the motivating factor seems to be fear – fear of the unknown, fear that reality will vastly outstrip established theory, fear that future experience will burst apart the nice, neat, well-understood boundaries that the experts attempt to set as a way of reducing the world of experience to some sort of comprehensible order and size. That fear then results in the elevation of the misconstrued axioms of basic theory into immovable cosmic barriers that none dare approach and that consequently become the ultimate taboos.

Though it has to be admitted that, for the native inhabitants of the Americas at least, Columbus's expeditions did indeed (as it happens) precipitate a descent into hell.

5. Further Deduction: Time dilation

Alternatively referred to as 'time dilatation', this deduction states that if two observers are moving at a constant velocity relative to each other, it appears to each that the other's time processes are slowed down. Once again, this effect increases with relative speed, so that at the observed relative speed of light the other's time appears to stop completely.

As ever, of course, this is a statement about appearance, not reality. Aboard each presumed spaceship, time would in fact appear to be ticking on at its usual 'petty pace'. Only aboard the *other* ship would time appear to have slowed.

Which is odd, since speed is *itself* a function of time, and is normally expressed in kilometres or miles *per hour* or *per second*. At the observed relative speed of light, then, each second would now last an eternity, *which inevitably means that the other ship's speed would now appear to be zero.*

But for the fact that it would in the meantime also have apparently thinned into nothingness, then, its ghost would now appear to be hanging forever motionless in space – even though it had in fact long since shot off into regions well beyond human ken.

One inevitable consequence of this deduction, incidentally, is that the light from a distant galaxy will appear to undergo a shift towards the red end of the spectrum if it is rapidly moving away from us. And, true enough, most of the galaxies in the night sky do appear to be redshifted. It was on this very fact that the famous American astronomer Edwin Hubble originally based his celebrated 'expanding universe' theory on which so much of modern cosmology is based. Unfortunately for the theory, however, Einsteinian time dilation means that a galaxy will undergo the self-same redshift if it is moving rapidly *towards us*, too. This of course spells disaster not only for Hubble's theory, but also for the consequent quasi-creationist mythology of Primeval Atom and Big Bang. But then, since this latter was originally proposed by a Belgian Roman Catholic priest by the name of Georges Lemaître,[18] we might in any case have suspected that it had more to do with re-clothing the ancient creationist teachings of the Church in modern garb than with likely scientific fact.

Once again, in other words, priestly surmisings had entered the field of factual argument – not, this time, in the field of history, but in that of science and cosmology. But this time they were accepted. A grateful establishment was in this case only too pleased to have its preconceptions apparently justified.

6. The Equivalence of Mass and Energy

This notion is most famously expressed by Einstein's celebrated equation $E = mc^2$, where E stands for energy, m for mass and c for the observed relative speed of light. What this means, in effect, is that a small amount of matter is equivalent to a huge amount of energy. And indeed, the proposition was amply proved, if proof were needed, by the explosion of the first atomic bomb.

This aspect of the theory arose as a direct consequence of Einstein's calculations of the perceived increase in mass of an object travelling at near-light speeds relative to the observer. Inevitably, he argued, that mass increase would be associated with an enormous amount of kinetic energy, or momentum – thanks primarily to the huge relative speed at which the object would have to be travelling to achieve the effect. The actual figures could be calculated. The fact that the increase in mass would be only a *perceived* increase in mass, and that the energy increase was consequently only a *perceived* energy increase, was neither here nor there, since both perceptions – both relativities – could now simply be 'cancelled out', so to speak, on both sides of the equation.

And certainly the upshot was real enough – real enough to kill well over 100,000 Japanese as a result of a single, terrifying explosion.

As a mathematical tool, then, relativity has its uses, nefarious or otherwise. It should not in itself be taken too literally, however. It tells us more about our perceptions than it does about the world out there. It seems to operate in a bewildering borderland where consciousness merges into motion, and motion into light. And it may yet turn out that all three are, in some strange and as yet ill-understood way, one and the same.

7. Proofs of the Special Theory

Apart from the truly cataclysmic demonstration of the atomic bomb, the claimed proofs of the Special Theory have, on the whole, been rather underwhelming to date. They have been based mainly on experiments suggesting that small atomic particles do indeed get heavier the faster they go. Atomic clocks have even been flown around the world in different directions and observed to differ from a third, static clock by minute amounts. It is widely deduced, then, that in both cases the observed changes were what actually happened.

But this, of course, is merely *as measured by the experimenters*. Nobody has yet managed to ask the particles involved whether *they themselves* feel heavier, or the clocks whether time has gone more slowly *for them*. Perhaps clocks and watches *always* seem to slow down during long air journeys.

Certainly mine always does.

The only way to find out what has *really* happened, then, would appear to be to fire off *the researchers* into space and see what *they* feel. The only problem with this, though, is that we shall probably never find out.

Possibly, though, we can guess.

THE GENERAL THEORY

First published in 1916, the General Theory of Relativity extends the Special Theory into the area of observed relative speeds *involving acceleration* and deals with several further, associated points.

1. The Principle of Equivalence

The principle of equivalence states that, at any given point in space, the effects of gravitation and accelerated motion are indistinguishable and therefore, for the purposes of relativity, equivalent.

As any pilot knows, for example, an aircraft set up to fly at 1 G (i.e. at normal Earth gravity – as experienced, for example, in straight and level flight) will continue to fly at 1 G *whatever its attitude*. Thus, should the pilot fall asleep in thick cloud and the aircraft inadvertently turn upside-down, he will not know from his immediate sense impressions that this has happened, since the aircraft will still be doing its best to maintain 1 G – *in this case by going into a rapidly steepening dive*. Only the instruments will initially tell him anything different. Many, indeed, are the disorientated young trainee pilots who have ploughed into the ground at night in this way because they thought that the lights on the ground were stars in the sky.

You may choose to believe this or not. But if you doubt that acceleration (which includes deceleration and change of direction, incidentally) is indistinguishable from gravity, try detaching your-self from the whirling Wall of Death the next time you come across a fairground.

2. The Effect of Gravity on Light

In view of 1. above, the second deduction states that travelling light beams are likely to be deflected (and thus 'accelerated') by gravitational fields such as those of stars and planets.

3. The Slowing Down of Time on Large Masses

This third deduction predicts that time – as represented by atomic clocks, for example – will be slower on large celestial bodies than on small ones. Since, in effect, atoms are *themselves* atomic clocks, this should be apparent in the shifting of light that reaches us from the sun, for example, towards the longer wavelengths, and thus towards the red end of the spectrum.

4. Proofs of the General Theory

All the deductions of the General Theory have duly been con-firmed by astronomical observations. This once again amounts to saying that what the Theory predicts as being perceived *is* per-ceived.

Which, once again, is no more than we might expect.

CONCLUSIONS FOR SPACE FLIGHT

The upshot of all this for space flight, then, is that faster-than-light travel is neither impossible nor taboo under the terms of Einstein's theory. Indeed, it is almost certainly inevitable. Those partaking in it need notice no relativistic effects at all unless they look out of the window or try to communicate with Earth. True, it will be important to steer well clear of large stars and planets, carefully balancing the projected course so as to be as equidistant as possible from all gravity fields. Because of the distortion of the external visual field, too, navigation will probably need to be exclusively inertial.

Apart from these points, however, the main problems will lie not in the field of Einsteinian metaphysics, but in the hard realities of life support and, above all, of propulsion systems. Yet even these are likely to be solved by the time the great Space Odyssey takes place – whether with outside assistance or without it.

Indeed, the big question at the time may well be not so much 'Dare we embark on this Great Adventure?' as 'Why embark on *this* particular one, rather than on one of the many others currently on offer?'

That is a question that the Elohim themselves will no doubt answer in truly emphatic terms.

20

SPACE
ODYSSEY
2499

IT IS 21 FEBRUARY 2499. The visiting Elohim have done their work. Whether in their natural form or through the agency of chosen, trained human beings (much as in the case, perhaps, of the former Moses), they have carefully prepared humanity for the Great Day. Minds have been opened, sensitivities awakened, restricting beliefs abandoned, capabilities immeasurably expanded. Humans have learnt through a process of occasionally painful trial and error to identify themselves with their planet, to work as one for its welfare, to become the true product of its maternal body – in short, to become the single, interconnected organism that the Hindus have always called *Purusha*, that the ancient Pharisees dubbed the *Logos* (or Man-Thought-in-the-Mind-of-God), and that we ourselves could perhaps call *Earthchild*.

As a result, humanity has at last become attuned to Earth, and Earth to the wider cosmos. Stunningly, the ancient gods have left us a schematic picture of this very outcome in the Great Pyramid's south elevation (*see diagram overleaf*). Here, from a southerly point representing the ultimate completion of the plan, the picture is of the perfected being who eventually emerges from the south face of the Pyramid – a man (the figure is quite definitely masculine) who is standing facing the west, with the fivefold crown of perfection on his head. While feet, genitals and stomach are all clearly identifiable, the emphasis is clearly on his *mind*, which has evidently undergone vast expansion, and the key to that expansion appears to be his tongue, as represented by the axially-placed King's Chamber coffer – in other words, his language.

That language has become the newly attuned song of Earth, that mind the instrument of its future destiny. As the passages are locked into the Pyramid, so humanity is locked into Earth. The two can henceforth proceed as one.

The human race has at last qualified to serve as Earth's ambassador to the rest of the universe.

And with that ultimate achievement the new, collective being that is Earthchild at last qualifies to be taught the great knowledge, the wisdom of the Elohim, the science of the greater universe. Dangerous technologies can be safely imparted – the technology necessary for penetrating deep space, for landing on innocent remote worlds, for contacting unsuspecting alien intelligences.

First on the list is necessarily the technology of constructing huge space arks, or generation starships. Put together in Earth orbit, these are, in effect, massive mobile living environments designed to house upward of a thousand people at a time. While they do not need to be streamlined, they probably *are* streamlined – purely in order to reduce the impact of minor particles in space. Alternatively some kind of deflector shield may be devised. Certainly *some* kind of shielding is essential to protect the future travellers from cosmic rays. For descending out of orbit on to planetary surfaces, the ships are of course provided with smaller space shuttles designed for atmospheric re-entry.

Inside, all the normal necessities of life are catered for. The environment is entirely self-supporting. Facilities are included for the manufacturing or growing of all food – possibly hydroponically – as well as for recycling all waste, be it exhaled carbon dioxide or the liquid and solid products of digestion. This means that there are plants, animals, gardens and/or farms, as well as parks and

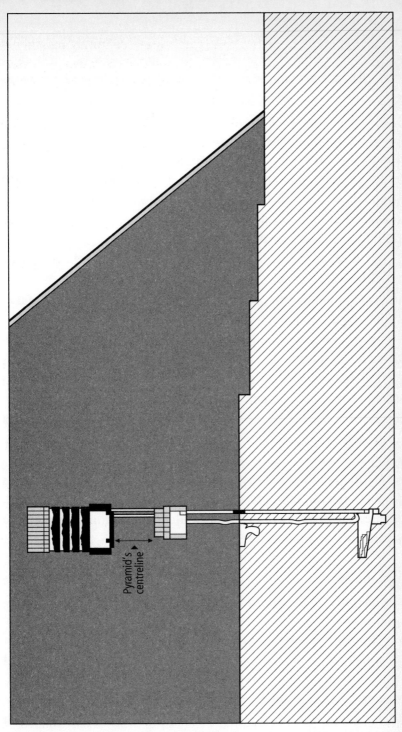

Elevation of the Great Pyramid's passage system, looking north

possibly even swimming pools for recreation. All the usual infra-structure of schools, universities, hospitals, morgues, workshops, factories, power stations and administrative quarters is also provid-ed for, on top of more than sufficient private accommodation – for people are necessarily going to have to live, die and breed *en route*, and their numbers may well grow.

Socially, preparations have also been made. Structures of gov-ernment and command have been set up. Structures of law have been laid down. Officers and crew of all ages have been appointed and passengers carefully selected – though many of them have no doubt selected themselves.

Nothing can be left to chance – for, once the ships have depart-ed, they will be entirely on their own *for generations*.

Possibly the biggest problem to be overcome, however, is that of propulsion. Various systems have already been proposed, ranging from the electromagnetic ion drive, through the laser-driven sail drive to the pulsed fusion drive. The problem with all of them is that of energy expenditure. Unless the ships can somehow extract energy from space itself, that energy will necessarily be limited. Unfortunately, the 'ramscoop' that has been proposed to collect hydrogen from space for this purpose is likely to slow the starship down at least as much as it speeds it up.

At this point, consequently, most of today's science-fictionists resort to the mighty 'spacedrive'. This is not always clearly defined. In the case of *Star Trek*, it is the result of the fusion of matter and antimatter, and takes the form of a 'warp drive' – a technique, in other words, that works by deforming spacetime itself. In effect, the ship either stays still or 'surfs' on a spacetime wave, while spacetime itself does most of the moving.

This at least appears to dispose of one major problem with the more powerful drives – namely that of acceleration. If the ship ac-celerates for any length of time at more than 1 G (the equivalent of normal Earth gravity), the results are likely to be fatal for pas-sengers and crew alike. Even a single, brief acceleration at more than a few G can prove disastrous, notwithstanding the fact that those involved are not only fit, but lying down relative to the direction of acceleration to prevent drainage of blood from the brain.

Much depends in this case, then, on the development of some kind of gravity control. Indeed, once this is developed, most of the propulsion problems disappear of their own accord. The ship can proceed simply by manipulating gravities *en route* – now using gravity to obtain the celebrated 'slingshot effect' by swinging around the back of some huge star or planet, now using *anti*gravity to push itself even more rapidly away from it into deep space.

The problems, it has to be admitted, sound rather daunting. Yet virtually all of today's great seers – Jeane Dixon and Mario de Sabato,[22] for example, to say nothing of Arthur C. Clarke[4] – assure us that the mighty spacedrive will indeed be developed, and will eventually result in our being able to cross the cosmos as easily as we now cross the seas.

What, then, are the requirements? How distant is our destination? What accelerations will be needed? How long will the journey take? For how many generations will those aboard the departing space arks have to continue living and dying and breeding before they eventually arrive for their awesome encounter with the Elohim Cloud in the neighbourhood of Al Nitak?

The figures are fairly straightforward. Al Nitak is currently calculated to lie some 1,100 light years from us – even though, as we have already seen, that is really only where it *used to be* 1,100 years ago. Taking the figure as our basis, at all events, the journey would take at least 1,100 years if we were restricted to the speed of light. As we noted in the previous chapter, however, light *has* no speed in any absolute sense. Consequently there is no such limitation. We can continuing accelerating to any speed we like, subject only to the natural limitations of the human body.

In practice, then – failing the eventual development of the much-vaunted gravity control – we are restricted to a steady, prolonged acceleration of 1 G (in mathematical terms, approximately 980 centimetres per second per second, or 32.16 feet per second per second). This will mean that everybody on board will be living in normal Earth gravity for the entire length of the trip. *Moreover, it*

is well within our current technology. Even the humble, everyday heli-
copter achieves 1 G every time it takes to the air. The problem lies
in (a) the size and consequent mass of the ship and (b) the length
of time for which that acceleration has to be maintained.

Let us look at what is involved. The likely distance, we have
seen, is some 1,100 light years. In order to arrive in the shortest
possible time, the ship is going to have to accelerate at 1 G until it
reaches the halfway point then, swinging about through 180 degrees (still at 1 G, which will throw it off course slightly, but can
easily be adjusted for subsequently), *de*celerate at the same, steady
1 G for the rest of the trip. It *could* of course choose to coast for
much of the journey. This, though, would not only take longer,
but expose those aboard to all the harmful, if heady effects of prolonged weightlessness into the bargain.

The mathematics are quite specific. At a steady acceleration
of 1 G, the speed of light (relative to the receding Earth) will be
reached after just over 353 days – i.e. perhaps surprisingly, *in
rather less than a year*. A speed relative to Earth of 10*c* will be
reached after just over 9½ years, by which time the ship will, at an
average relative speed of 5*c* since it started out, have covered a
distance of nearly 50 light years. The halfway point of 550 light
years will be reached during year 33 of the voyage – by which time
a relative speed of some 33*c* will have built up. The long process of
*de*celeration will then have to begin – still at a steady 1 G – with
the result that the travellers will finally arrive in the neighbourhood of Al Nitak *some 65 Earth-years after they started out*.

But 65 years is a long time. It is the equivalent of nearly three
generations. True, the Great Pyramid allows all of 490 years for the
great Odyssey. But who knows whether the vision that inspired
the original pioneers will continue to be maintained throughout
the trip? Possibly the presence of the accompanying Elohistic en-
voys will help, but it is still a pretty tall order.

Much will therefore hinge on the development of a more powerful spacedrive and appropriate gravity control technology. If this
can be achieved, then much higher accelerations will be able to be
reached and the journey time correspondingly shortened. Indeed,

were the technology to be developed only *after* the departure of the original pioneers, their descendants might well find their Earth cousins already waiting for them when they finally arrived.

On the whole this seems unlikely, however. The signs are that the Elohim will see to it that all the technology is mastered well before the day of initial departure.

And so it is that the Great Exodus will duly begin on time, and humanity will go to meet the Elohim in the far distant clouds of the galaxy. Even then, of course, the journey will not finally be over. The pioneers will have to remain aboard while the great merging of consciousness takes place – possibly using some kind of neuro-magnetic technology – then continue on their way to their ultimate destination.

Who knows where that destination will be? Who knows, indeed, *who they* will by then be? The being that arrives on the ultimate planet, after all, will be a collective being with many arms and legs *but a single Higher Mind*. It will feel feelings and think thoughts that you and I would not even be able to recognize as such.

True, that being will be forever beyond the light of our sun, but it will not have been cast into outer darkness. Indeed, it will have an entirely new sun to bathe it. Its life, consequently will be renewed. It will be a new humanity. And, much as the Bible's *Book of Revelation* reveals, it will need neither temple nor religion, for it will already be in direct contact with the Elohim themselves.

Indeed, it will actually *be* the Elohim.

And as such it will go on to achieve its promised bliss on a new Earth, under a new heaven.

21

AFTERWORD:
BEYOND
ALL
BELIEF

IN THIS BOOK I HAVE DARED to think the unthinkable – largely because there would have been little point in thinking what everybody has thought before. But this very fact means that everybody can find something in it to object to.

The unthinking, of course, will not think about it at all. If they do not take the whole thing simply on trust, they will simply dismiss it as incomprehensible – *quite literally* unthinkable – having no more substance (and about as much sense) as a dream. Their objections will therefore be entirely understandable.

The intellectual and cultural dinosaurs – conventional thinkers who believe that they already know all the answers – will accuse me of spouting credulous nonsense, notwithstanding the fact that they will be hard put to it to find facts that are not as claimed or details that are incorrect. The violence of their language, in fact, will reveal the precise extent to which their preconceptions have been offended.

Even enthusiasts of my own previous books, who possibly believe that they contain all the answers they want, may well berate me for going well beyond the spiritual or psychological pale that they see them as setting. Here I can only reply that that was then, and this is now. Truth is yesterday, today and forever, and it is no more exclusively spiritual or psychological than it is physical or astronomical. Truth, in short, is truth, and as such it necessarily encompasses all areas of our experience whenever and however we experience them.

Many science fiction enthusiasts, on the other hand, who believe that everything is possible, will criticize me for not going nearly far enough. It is not just a matter of failing to mention the Little Green Men (of whatever size and colour). Where, they will ask, is that Ultimate Cosmic Intelligence that has by now transformed itself into a sheer lattice of light, imprinting itself on the very warp and woof of space time itself? The answer is of course that I have found no trace of encounters with such an intelligence in the specific destiny spelt out for us in the passages and chambers of the Great Pyramid, whatever even greater encounters may be in store for us subsequently.

The religious, for their part, who for the most part believe what they are told, will condemn the book as a travesty of the truth, accusing me of wilfully appropriating their own terms and concepts to construct a vision of the future that is, in effect, a diabolical caricature. But then in their case it is their very beliefs – their prior assumptions, in other words – that, like ill-fitting blinkers, will ensure that they will be the last people to recognize the truth that they have always believed in when it finally stares them in the face. So that, even if this happened to be it, they would certainly deny it...

This is always the function of statements of belief. In the very act of defining what we believe, they also define what we do *not* believe. And since what we believe can only ever be a very small part of what *is*, we thereby rule out the overwhelming balance of probabilities, whether for our present or for our future. The long story of the steady disappearance of God in the face of expanding scientific knowledge offers more than ample evidence of this. Belief, in short, is merely our way of making the world conceptually safe for ourselves. It rules out the unknown. It abolishes the unexpected. It banishes the unthinkable.

Yet as I said earlier, it is precisely the unthinkable that I have dared to think in this book. To that extent it goes beyond all conventional belief. In the final upshot, though, something rather surprising has happened. The unthinkable has paradoxically turned out to be – if in surprising and disturbing ways – remarkably similar to what has always been thought before. Indeed, it is precisely the extent to which this book's outline of humanity's future destiny turns out to mirror the immemorial beliefs of antiquity that is most likely to worry the religious in particular.

It is as if we always knew what the eventual outcome might be. Some seed, planted in our ancient consciousness by who knows whom, long ago gave us an inkling of the end of the story even before we knew how to begin it.

That, of course, is how visions work. They posit a goal and erect a signpost. They do not tell us how to put one foot in front of the other. They do not tell us what to believe. They do not tell us what dragons and precipices we shall encounter. Often they do not even tell us how far it is to our goal.

Yet where there is no vision (as the Authorized Version of the Bible incorrectly but perspicaciously translates it) the people perish.

The ancient signpost of imagination whose finger we have been following is one such. It is a signpost that has led from the twilight of the last ice age, by way of the dawn of pre-dynastic Egypt and the sunrise of Greece, via the respective lights of classical Rome and the much later European Renaissance to the blinding lightning flashes of the atomic era and the space age.

And its function has always been to face us with the inconceivable and present us with the impossible. Its message has been that we are limited only by our own imaginations, hemmed in only by our own beliefs.

In the event, we have gone on to learn both – the hard way. The ancient message has been first ritualized, then questioned, then ignored, then forgotten, then encountered anew. What should have set us free has been turned into religions that have bamboozled us, dogmas that have enslaved us, mumbo-jumbo that has passed us by, then new babblings that have invited our credulity all over again.

But the real function of the Elohistic initiative, if I have reconstructed it aright, is not to subject us to beliefs that shackle us, but to blast apart our imagined limitations. Its purpose is not to enchain us, but to set us free – not by telling us, like most religions, what we cannot do, but by hinting, however remotely, at what we can.

Somehow it has managed to adumbrate what the world's religions have only managed dimly to foreshadow – that humanity's potential is unlimited provided that we let go of our self-imposed limitations, that our greater identity is served only by identifying ourselves with each other and with our world, that we have a destiny that is not confined to Planet Earth, that there are friendly intelligences elsewhere in the universe, and that our consciousness may yet be raised to levels beyond our wildest dreams.

In all this, imagination is the key. That is what visions are about. The future described by the Great Pyramid has something of the substance of a dream. To this extent, at least, my unthinking critics will be right, and possibly nearer to the truth than most.

The humanity of the future may well encounter the mooted superior beings 'out there'. But it will also have encountered a dream in the mind of man – or of the universe. For dreams, too, can take on concrete form. Light, motion, relativity and the whole of the perceived universe are all dreams, all functions of human consciousness. If there is a universe beyond our perceiving we cannot perceive it. Even the Elohim themselves are a dream made manifest.

Though who the original Dreamer was is, of course, not apparent to those within the dream itself.

Dreams in due course become reality. What we dream today we experience tomorrow. The science-fictionists, no less than the scientists, are the creators of our future. Let them take care, then, what they dream. For mind is the maker of worlds. Yet, just as in the case of the atomic bomb, it can be their dissolver, too.

Mind – the selfsame Mind that we share with the Elohim and with all other sentient beings – is Brahma the Creator. It is Shiva the Destroyer. It is blue Vishnu in the sky, Orion in the flesh, the starry bones of God, the forger of destiny, the embodier of all that humanity has ever been and is ever likely to become.

Lovers, O lovers! Lo, the time has come
This world to leave, for now from heaven on high
My spirit's ear detects the parting drum.
The driver's up, the camel train stands by
And now he begs us for indemnity.
Why still asleep, then, travellers? O why?

...Each moment sees a soul and spirit fly
Into the void, for from these stars so bright
Like candles hanging down, and from the sky
Whose awnings blue bedrape the lofty height
Has come a wondrous race whose quest divine
Is to reveal the mysteries aright.

...O watchman, wake! sleep ill becomes your post:
In every street shouting and tumult reign.
Of lamps and torches stir a thronging host.
Tonight the seething Earth awakes again
To bring the world eternal forth to birth.
Dull dust you were, wise spirit shall remain.

Jalal'ud-Din Rumi (1207–73): from Dîwān-i Shams-i Tabriz

REFERENCE – BIBLIOGRAPHY

1) Bauval, R. and Gilbert, A.: *The Orion Mystery* (Heinemann, 1995)

2) Bauval, R. and Hancock, G.: *Keeper of Genesis* (Heinemann, 1996)

3) Burke, J.: *The Day the Universe Changed* (BBC, 1985)

4) Clarke, A. C.: *Profiles of the Future* (Gollancz, 1962; Pan, 1964)

5) Coleman, J.A.: *Relativity for the Layman* (Penguin, 1959)

6) Cottrell, L.: *The Lost Pharaohs* (Evans, 1950: Pan, 1956)

7) Davidson, D. and Aldersmith, J.: *The Great Pyramid: Its Divine Message* (Williams & Norgate, 1925)

8) Edwards, I.E.S.: *The Pyramids of Egypt* (Penguin, 1980)

9) Einstein, A.: *Relativity: The Special and the General Theory* (Methuen, 1920)

10) Fakhry, A.: *The Pyramids* (University of Chicago, 1961)

11) Flem-Ath, R. & R.: *When the Sky Fell* (Weidenfeld & Nicolson, 1995; Orion, 1996)

12) Grimal, P. (ed.): *Larousse World Mythology* (Hamlyn, 1973)

13) Hancock, G., *Fingerprints of the Gods* (Heinemann, 1995)

14) Henbest, N. & Marten, M.: *The New Astronomy* (Cambridge U.P, 1983)
15) Hoyle, F.: *The Black Cloud* (Heinemann, 1957)
16) Jeans, Sir J.: *The Universe Around Us* (Cambridge U.P., 1930)
17) Jowett, B. (tr.): *The Dialogues of Plato*. Vol. 3 (Sphere, 1970)
18) Lemesurier, P.: *Beyond All Belief* (Element, 1983)
19) Lemesurier, P.: *The Great Pyramid Decoded* (Element, 1977)
20) Lemesurier, P.: *The Great Pyramid: Your Personal Guide* (Element, 1987)
21) Lemesurier, P.: *Nostradamus – The Next 50 Years* (Piatkus, 1993)
22) Lemesurier, P.: *Nostradamus: The Final Reckoning* (Piatkus, 1995)
23) Lemesurier, P.: *This New Age Business* (Findhorn, 1990)
24) Lunan, D.: *Man and the Stars: Contact and Communication with Other Intelligence* (Souvenir, 1974)
25) McIntosh, C.: *The Rosy Cross Unveiled* (Aquarian, 1980)
26) Moore, P.: *The A-Z of Astronomy* (Fontana, 1976)
27) Moore, P.: *The Guinness Book of Astronomy* (Guinness, 1979)
28) Mörner, N.A., Lanser, J.P. and Hospers, J., in *New Scientist*, 6th January 1972
29) Nichols, P. (ed.): *The Science in Science Fiction* (Michael Joseph, 1982)
30) Nostradamus, M.: *Lettre à Henry roy de France second*, printed with the *Propheties* of 1568 (Benoist Rigaud, Lyon)
31) Piazzi Smyth, C.: *Our Inheritance in the Great Pyramid* (1864)
32) Plato: *Timaeus*
33) Ridpath, I. & Tirion, W.: *Night Sky* (HarperCollins, 1985)
34) *Rig Veda, The*, tr. O'Flaherty, W.D. (Penguin, 1981)
35) Rutherford, A.: *Pyramidology*, Books 1–4 (Institute of Pyramidology, 1957 onwards)
36) Sabato, M. de: *Confidences d'un voyant* (Hachette, 1971)
37) Sitchin, Z.: *The Stairway to Heaven* (Avon, 1980)
38) Smith, W.: Strata *Identified by Organised Fossils* (1814)
39) Tompkins, P.: *Secrets of the Great Pyramid* (Allen Lane, 1973)
40) Ussher, J.: *Annals of the World* (1650)

INDEX